*Villa on the Shore*

# Villa on the Shore

## MICHAEL BUTTERWORTH

PUBLISHED FOR THE CRIME CLUB BY
DOUBLEDAY & COMPANY, INC.
GARDEN CITY, NEW YORK
1974

All of the characters in this book
are fictitious, and any resemblance
to actual persons, living or dead,
is purely coincidental.

Library of Congress Cataloging in Publication Data

Butterworth, Michael, 1924–
  Villa on the shore.

  I. Title.
PZ4.B9883Vi3      [PR6052.U9]      823'.9'14
ISBN: 0-385-08794-2
Library of Congress Catalog Card Number 73–9014

TO MY CHILDREN:
*Sally, Nick, Deborah,*
*Polly, Candida, and Natasha*

*Villa on the Shore*

# 1

The newsagent's kiosk in the hall of the airport reception building carried a display of Nathan Yardley's sensational best seller, and Natasha bought a copy. Her earlier inclination to wait till it came out in paperback was suddenly revealed to her as being—considering the circumstances—picayune to an almost laughable degree, and having read it in condensed form as a newspaper serial really didn't count. She also bought a lunchtime edition of the *Courier,* after first checking the front page to see if there had been a gruesome air disaster during the morning. There had not. Another British business-man had been arrested in Peking, a Parisian housewife had produced stillborn sextuplets, and there was the rumblings of a dock strike. All was well with the world—in the area of pas-senger aviation.

It's simply, she later told her reflection in the mirrored wall behind the bar, that I have back trouble. She giggled, and nearly choked on her dry martini. When it comes to flying, she explained to herself, I have a yellow streak down my back. There are no jokes like the old jokes. Her reflection looked back at her: tall, slim, brown-eyed—and it was one of those days when her nose, which was widely described as aristo-cratic, was resolutely deciding to be prominent, merely.

She had another drink—and that had to last till Naples, for there was no telling who would be waiting to pick her up at the airport. When her flight was called, she walked the long corridor and tried not to see the silvery liners nuzzling, like baby whales at their mother, down each side of the block. But there was no shutting out the eldritch screams of the jets, and the dry martinis might never have been.

She was given a gangway seat, next to a grey-haired little woman, who eyed her from head to foot and put a price ticket on all her clothes. Then they turned on the engines and shut the door with a muffled clump. She assembled a phrase: hermetically sealed coffin—and felt her skin crawl at the aptness of it. A hostess murmured to her to fasten her seat belt, and—checking her nationality—gave her an immigration card to fill in.

This was a blessed bonus: a job of work to see her through the nightmare of the take-off.

NATASHA CYPRIAN COLLINGWOOD she wrote carefully and slowly in studiedly round, schoolgirlish capitals. SUDBURY, SUFFOLK, though how my place of birth could be of the slightest interest to the government of the Italian republic is beyond all belief. There was a leaden feeling in the pit of her stomach as the plane began to taxi forward.

Despite an elaborate protraction of her task, the filling-in of the card saw her only to the queue of aircraft at the end of the runway. Moments later, she was focussing closely on the front page of her newspaper; trying to shut out the sight of the grass verge flickering past the corner of her eye, and the inertia that was pressing her firmly back into her seat.

Mme. Madeleine Dupuis, she read fixedly, was thirty-six and had been taking fertility drugs under hospital supervision. This was the first recorded sextuplet birth in the Department of Paris-Seine. Mme. Dupuis was reported to be . . .

She fantasied herself as Madeleine Dupuis in the labour ward when the midwife broke the news, and when she asked to see them, the woman pointed to a steel-topped table at the other side of the ward, where six little forms lay in line, all covered with sheets, like the victims surrounding a crashed airliner. . . .

She switched hastily to the story of Mr. Ernest Bottomley, forty-one, who was arrested at his Peking flat yesterday and taken to some place unknown. There are now three British businessmen being held, without trial or formal charges, in Red China. The others are Mr. David Eaves, thirty-three, and Mr. W. O. Spurgeon, forty-eight, who were both . . .

She was Ernest Bottomley in his narrow cell, with Eaves and Spurgeon heaven knows where in the same building. It was stiflingly hot and Bottomley was stripped naked. Naked, he was lying on the bunk, which was nothing more than a bare concrete slab . . . like they have in a mortuary. . . .

"Did you say something, dear?" It was the woman at her elbow. "I quite thought you called out, but I'm a bit deaf this side. It's all right to take your seat belt off now, you know."

They were up high, and everything was very still and curiously not fear-provoking. Central London was below them: She could make out Lord's Cricket Ground and the glint of the canal in Regent's Park. Natasha relaxed, let the newspaper slip to the floor, and took the book from her zipper bag.

*Nathan Yardley*
*PRIDE GOES BEFORE*

There was no illustration on the jacket; only the title and the author's name on a matt, black background. Natasha read the blurb on the inside flap:

Once in a decade, or less often, a truly great novel streaks like a comet across the sky of publishing, putting all the established stars to shame. Such a novel is PRIDE GOES BEFORE. Reviewers have been quick to discover "a superb work of craftsmanship" (Robin Gray, *Evening Courier*) and "a masterly first novel which, in one bound, establishes Nathan Yardley among the immortals" (Nicholas Randall, *The Globe*), and "must certainly become the best seller of the '70s" (Derek Vessey, *Northern Union*).

Yardley's theme is destruction: man's destruction of his own environment, of his fellow-man, of his own immortal soul. . . .

She flipped the book over. His picture was on the back of the dust jacket: a lean, heavily tanned face shaded under a casual straw hat; humorous wrinkles at the mouth, quirky lips. His frame was big and spare under the sweat-shirt. No middle-aged flab, though his dark hair was heavily peppered with grey about his ears. He's always seemed to me, thought Natasha, the sort of person who would be a tower of strength in a lifeboat.

There was a potted biography under the picture:

Nathan Yardley was born in Birmingham, and is forty-three years old. British TV viewers remember him as one of the leading stars of the successful *Tell Me Another One Do* panel game of the late '60s. PRIDE GOES BEFORE, which took Mr. Yardley ten years to write, has already been translated into twelve languages and is at the moment being filmed by R. G. C. Associates. Mr. Yardley is widowed, with two stepchildren, and spends most of the year in Italy.

Then there was the opening of the book, which had already found its way into all the trendiest dictionaries of quotations the world over. She read it with a smile.

### Chapter One

I've lain under the Southern Cross with a nut-brown maid, seen the Sugar Loaf towering out of the sea of mist of Rio Bay, blown three months' salary in one night of Monte Carlo, been broke in Cochin, pissed up against the Golden Gates of Samarkand. . . .

The woman next to her was laughing. She jogged Natasha's elbow and nodded down at the book.

"Did you ever read anything so brazen?" she said. "It has me in fits every time I think about it. My hubby and I have both read the book, of course. We're in the retail tobacconist and confectionary trade, so it's never convenient to take our summer hols together, and I do so like to get away in May before the Continent's all jammed with tourists. We were great followers of Nathan's on "Tell Me Another One Do." He lives not far from Capri, you know—which is where I'm going."

"He lives near Amalfi," corrected Natasha. Then, as casually as she was able: "I'm on my way to join him right now, as his new secretary."

The woman turned suddenly arch and affronted: not believing Natasha, and scarcely bothering to hide the fact. Freed of the burden of her conversation, Natasha was able to skip-read the first few chapters of the book, while filling-in with self-congratulatory recollections of how she had—so suddenly and surprisingly—become the author's employee.

For she had not lied to the woman. Returning home from a weekend in the country with relations, she had found her flat-mate, Veronica, in a tizzy of excitement. The very exclusive secretarial agency (graduates only) with whom they were both registered, had just rung up, offering Natasha the job with Nathan Yardley—this on account of the fact that she had done so splendidly in coping with the tantrums of a lady thriller-writer who had severed her connections, with Natasha and this world, with an overdose of barbiturates, only a month before. Natasha's file had been marked: "marvellous with authors." She could also speak Italian. A seat had been booked on the Naples-bound plane for Wednesday, and the ticket and cash for expenses would be delivered by hand if she accepted the job. Natasha telephoned immediately and accepted it.

She turned the book over and had another look at the face on the back of the dust jacket.

Authorship aside, Yardley's TV reputation—like so many others—had not been founded on the display of sweetness and light, but on the exercising of a real or simulated abrasiveness. The viewing public had loved Yardley for being outspoken in confrontation with elements whose ideas it had become unfashionable to question: he had mocked the trendy Left, contradicted the Young, tongue-lashed the Permissive. On the other hand, he had ducked out from under the mantle of reaction by kissing a leader of Women's Lib and shaking hands with a prominent homosexual.

You're a bit of an unknown quantity, thought Natasha. But I'm keeping my fingers crossed that life with you isn't going to be anything like it was with poor Mimi Middleton.

The sky had been overcast all the way from Naples, hiding the crest of Vesuvius. Now the clouds were massing over the hilly spine of the peninsula; somewhere up there, thunder was rumbling among the patchwork of vineyards and lemon groves.

It was nearly four o'clock. There was not much traffic on the winding cliff road. The taxi driver brought his off-side wheels on to the pavement opposite a high limewashed wall and wrought-iron gates, snicked on the handbrake, and put on his peaked cap again.

"This is the Villa Gaspari?" asked Natasha, pointing.

"*Si, si, signorina.*" The man had remained resolutely uncommunicative from the moment he had met her at the airport with her name chalked on a board and held in front of his chest.

The wrought-iron gates were somehow fastened on the inside, and backed with wooden boards—presumably for privacy's sake. It was impossible to see anything of the villa or its grounds. The driver hammered on the boards and shouted. After a while, it brought a drawing-back of bolts. The gates opened, and there was a barefoot young girl in her mid-teens standing there. Behind her was the sea and the sky, stretching to an infinity of distance. And below her, the rooftops of the Villa Gaspari, descending the stepped cliff to where the breakers washed among the rocks.

"Hello," smiled Natasha encouragingly. "I'm Natasha Collingwood, and you're expecting me."

The girl had—quite palpably—been crying. She made no reply, but stooped and picked up one of the cases. The taxi driver took the other, and nodded to Natasha to precede him down the balustraded steps that led to a tiled terrace flanked on each side by a row of cypresses.

When they got down there, she could see the main form of the villa and its incomparable setting. It looked old, but how old she had no competence to judge. Parts of it were rather grand, the lower part particularly, with a portico topped by Graeco-Roman statues. Other pieces of the villa looked more homely, all limewashed stone and terra cotta pantiles. There was no order about it; the separate parts simply clung to the cliffside as if they had always been there. A stone staircase snaked downwards, through light and shade, past old walls hung with jasmine, honeysuckle, and oleander, pausing by wide terraces and small, cool courtyards. And, as a backdrop to it all, the great sweep of the sea.

"It's so beautiful," said Natasha.

The driver made no comment, and the girl was some way

ahead of them, down the steps. She stopped a little farther down, by an archway, and looked back. When Natasha reached her, she elbowed open a door and gestured towards the room beyond.

"This is your room, *signorina.*"

There was a single bed with a carved tester canopy, a writing desk, and a button-back chair. The floor of the bedroom was tiled in blue and white. A single, large window looked directly out to sea, and its Venetian blinds were open.

Natasha tipped the driver and he left. The girl opened a door at the end, revealing a bathroom. She persisted in avoiding Natasha's eyes.

"Will that be all, *signorina?*"

"Is Mr. Yardley at home at the moment?" asked Natasha.

"No, *signorina.*"

"Or any of the family?"

"No, *signorina.* But they should be back any moment. I will tell you as soon as they arrive." She gave a little bobbing bow and went out.

Natasha started to unpack, hanging up her frocks in a fitted wardrobe that extended halfway along the room, opposite the window. It was while she was carrying her make-up and toilet things into the bathroom that she became aware of a curious scraping sound coming from somewhere below the open window. When she came out of the bathroom, she crossed over and looked out and downwards.

There was a small courtyard about forty feet below, enclosed by what seemed to be the rear of the villa's kitchen quarters: A small stack of cordwood and an array of empty wine bottles, and three tired-looking hens were scratching the dry earth bordering the plain flagstones of the yard.

Immediately under her window was the crouching figure of a grey-haired old man in a rusty black velvet waistcoat. He had a wooden bucket of water and what looked like a large block of pumice stone. With both hands on the pumice, he was working it back and forth across a patch of wet flagstone. After a while, he laid the pumice aside and examined the result of his labours: squatting on his haunches, head cocked; waiting till the patch of water had swiftly dried in the warmth, to disclose a rusty stain on the almost-white flagstone.

Then, with a growl of impatience, he addressed himself again to the task of obliterating the offending stain.

By this time, the sun had come out from behind the overcast, and Natasha decided she must make the most of its benefits.

To the left of her, the sweep of the gulf faded into a blue haze, with only pinpoints of white to describe the southern end of Salerno, under the distant mountains. A fishing boat was shaping a slanting course in that direction, trailing a mackerel-like wake after it on the glassy surface of the sea.

She was at the highest point of the Villa Gaspari: the upper terrace immediately below the entrance gates. Sitting, in a blue-and-white striped sun dress, on a stone bench under the cypresses. At a quarter to five, someone gave a commanding rattle at the gates. This brought a shout of acknowledgement from somewhere down in the kitchen quarters. But Natasha was already mounting the steps to the gates, two at a time. She drew back the heavy bolt, and the gate creaked open— to show her a face that had quickened innumerable Tuesday nights of British television. It was a face bronzed almost to the colour of chestnut, from which the eyes looked out at her with startling blueness. Nathan Yardley was hatless, and he wore a black light-weight suit and black knitted silk tie. He looked tired.

"Hello," she said. "I'm Natasha Collingwood," and gave him her hand.

Yardley seemed put out by the unexpected confrontation, and murmured an awkward phrase of greeting. Natasha's impression was of a man less sure of himself, and more kindly, than the man of the TV image.

"The others are on their way down," he said, looking back across the road.

She had not noticed it before, but there was a narrow cleft in the hillside a few yards from where her driver had parked the taxi. In it, rising steeply between dry stone walls, was a flight of worn steps that led up to the skyline, high above them. Two black-clad figures—a girl and a youth—were picking their way down the steps, deep in shadow.

"I'd hoped it would have been over before you arrived," said Nathan Yardley, "but it all took much longer than I'd anticipated. I hope they showed you to your quarters and made you comfortable."

"Yes, thank you."

"Well, that's all right then."

"It's a lovely place," she said.

The approaching couple were close enough, now, for her to make out their details. The girl was in her late teens, with blond hair worn long and straight, and darkly tanned skin. She swung down the steps with careless, gipsy-like grace, and her long black dress showed off her slenderness. The boy was younger—no more than a schoolboy—and he was following a dozen steps behind. He had the same butter-yellow hair cut short back and sides: There was no mistaking them for anything but siblings.

"My stepchildren," said Yardley.

There was Amanda. Close up, her dress was grubby, and she was barefoot. She pretended not to see Natasha's proffered hand, but looked past her and addressed the girl who had just come up from the kitchen to open the gate.

"Giulietta, did you remember to wash out those things for me?"

"*Si, signorina.*"

There was Eric. He took her hand and blushed like a girl. Every inch the British public schoolboy in his dark, clerical grey suit and heavy black shoes. Nice-looking, but rather spotty.

"Did you enjoy your walk?" asked Natasha, to fill a gaping hole in the conversation.

The question fell among them like a slow-fused fire-cracker. Eric's eyes widened, and he looked at his step-father as if for guidance. Yardley paused in the act of slotting home the bolt of the gate, turning slowly to stare at Natasha. The blond girl halted in mid-stride.

They were all staring at her now.

"Doesn't she know what's happened?" exclaimed Amanda.

"Be quiet!" snapped Yardley.

"I'm afraid I don't . . ." faltered Natasha.

"She *doesn't* know!" There was a note of malicious amusement in Amanda's voice.

Yardley made a wide gesture that encompassed the girl Giulietta. "But, surely, someone must have told you where we've been. You speak Italian, don't you?"

Natasha stared at him, bemused.

"We're dressed like this," explained Amanda, "because we've been to a funeral. The girl who had the job before you, suddenly gave a month's notice last Saturday, and then antic-ipated her departure the night before last—anticipated her departure somewhat precipitately, to coin a phrase. . . ."

"Amanda!"

"Oh, do me a favour, Nathan," retorted the girl. "I'm not

going to get all mealy-mouthed about Susannah at this stage."

Nathan Yardley's eyes held Natasha's. He seemed to be willing her to shut out Amanda's voice.

"It was all very sudden," he said quietly. "I should have sent a wire to my agent, to have you informed. I'm surprised the papers back home haven't picked up the story."

Amanda was not to be shut out: She seemed to be enjoying herself.

"Hang about," she said. "The reporters will be swarming here like flies round a honey pot as soon as anyone digs that you're involved."

"What happened to her?" asked Natasha.

"She fell out of her bedroom window," said Amanda.

With a sharp stab of horror, Natasha remembered the old man toiling, with a pumice stone, to clean away the rust-coloured stain.

"She was buried in a hurry," continued the girl. "They don't keep long in this climate. Corpses, I mean."

2

Nathan Yardley and his stepchildren were separately swal-
lowed up in the labyrinthine Villa Gaspari, and she was left
on her own again. There was presumably to be an evening
meal, but no one volunteered any information about when
or where. She would have liked to have had a chat with her
employer, followed perhaps by an informal conducted tour of
the place. It would have been nice, she thought, if he had
taken the trouble to have softened the shock of the grotesque
revelation about the girl—Susannah Hislop—whom they had
buried that afternoon. She rationalised his shortcoming by
supposing that the girl's death must have affected him, and he
did not want to talk about it. Then she decided to go for a
walk.

She put a linen stole about her shoulders and let herself out
of the gate.

The road looked dusty and as hot as a canyon. The steps
in the shadowy cleft opposite, down which Yardley and his
stepchildren had come, looked invitingly cool. It presumably
also led up to a high viewpoint, with a sensational view of the
Gulf of Salerno. She crossed the road and began to climb the
steps, which were quite wide, and flanked with towering dry-
stone walls overhung with broad-leaved fig trees drooping
with heavy purple fruit. Something moved among the weeds
by the wall's edge ahead of her, and next instant the whip-like

end of a black snake's tail slid smoothly into a cranny in the dry-stone. The chirruping of cicadas was everywhere, and continuous.

Before she was half way up the steps—and the top ended in a patch of blue sky framed by two giant pines, high above— she was hot and out of breath. The entrance to the cemetery was masked from view till she came upon it: high iron gates set in a recessed archway in the wall, and a break in the steps where sweating pallbearers would just have room to shuffle their burden round to face the entrance.

She looked in through the gates, and into a small, walled amphitheatre, silent and empty; set with gravestones, crosses of wrought iron, and little mausoleums, all guarded by dark, sentinel cypresses.

The high squeal of rusty hinges was contained and amplified by the surrounding walls, and all the uncountable cicadas fell silent, for a few instants, at the sound of it, then took up their chirruping again. She closed the gate behind her, to lessen the sense of intrusion.

The cemetery was laid out formally, with a path up the centre, and another making a circuit close to the walls. After a moment's indecision, she turned right and began to walk slowly round the amphitheatre, past the talismans of the dead, past the rusting iron and the sun-whitened stone, past the regarding eyes staring out at her from fading portrait photographs.

Then she came upon the fresh grave.

The red earth had been newly turned and newly put back. There was no headstone, no cross; only a wreath of dark laurel leaves and waxy arum lilies. Wired to a crosspiece in the center of the wreath was a cheap plastic photo frame, glazed with perspex. In it was a coloured snapshot of a girl with red hair and very pale skin. She was smiling rather self-consciously, as if someone had just prompted her.

And there was a black-edged card:

*In Deepest Sympathy from*
*Nathan Yardley and Family*

So this was Susannah Hislop. Natasha searched the out-of-focus features for a clue as to character and temperament, but nothing came across.

A slight breeze ruffled the pointed tips of the cypresses, and Natasha shivered, unconsciously drawing her stole more closely about her despite the heat. She felt the need to move on.

There was another way out of the cemetery: some steps at the far end that perhaps promised a quicker ascent to the plateau above; and indeed so it seemed, for when she reached the foot of the steps the summit was quite near.

She climbed out of the prim, silent cemetery till it was lost from her sight by its enclosing walls, and only the tops of the cypresses showed. And now she was so high up that, looking back, the great spread of the sea filled half of her world, and the sky the other half.

She paused three steps from the top and looked back again. Countless small sounds were coming up to her through the heat-haze: distant voices down by the water's edge; a car labouring round the hairpin bends of the cliff road; a fishing boat's motor far out at sea; a child's laugh; the endless cicadas.

And, as she stood there, it came quite clearly—the squeal of the cemetery gates being swung open.

Three steps more and she was on a rocky plateau set with dusty pines. Beyond, the vineyards and lemon groves stretched, tier upon tier, to the hillcrest that nearly touched the feathery clouds massing over the peninsula.

Natasha chose a smooth spot and, spreading out her stole like a rug, she lay down and closed her eyes.

A sense of unease preceded her awakening: Her dream carried overtones of some nameless intrusion. She sat up with a start, and her hands flew, instinctively, to guard her throat.

"Who's there? Who is it?" she cried.

Nothing and no one; only a gentle splattering of rain on her bare arms. The sky was overcast, and the line of the horizon was lost, so that sea and sky were all one. Her watch told her it was seven-fifteen. She had been asleep for over an hour, and the cicadas were silent.

The unease persisted, overlaid with a pang of anxiety about being late back at the villa and getting into disfavour with her new employer. She scooped up her stole, and set off down the steps leading to the cemetery. The stonework was wet and slippery under her sandalled feet. But the rain shower slackened when she reached the bottom and turned the corner of the wall.

Ahead of her lay the path that went past the grave of Susannah Hislop. At the far end of the walled amphitheatre were the gates—and one of them was wide open.

There was no one in the cemetery: No black-clad shape stooped in mourning.

She saw the scattered flecks of light and dark on the path ahead of her, and even before her mind had encompassed the wild improbability of what they might signify, she found herself beginning to tremble. The unease that had begun, in a sleeping state, up on the plateau among the pine trees, was now taking on the hard edges of a dreadful reality.

Susannah Hislop's grave had been violated.

The light and dark were the scattered remains of the wreath: leaves and flowers wrenched apart and strewn widely. Some of the lilies had even been torn into strips, and their stems ground underfoot, so that the stone path was stained with their juices.

The plastic snapshot holder lay in the middle of the path. She picked it up and turned it over, and was instantly nauseated.

The perspex glazing had been wrenched off, and the eyes in the snapshot had been burnt out. As if by a lighted cigarette end.

## 3

Two expensive-sounding car horns were blaring a duet in the road outside the villa, and she saw them when she had finished her headlong race down the steep steps: fast-back sportsters festooned with young people, and they were all shouting and hooting outside the locked gates for Amanda.

Amanda came out. She was wearing a patterned, ankle-length frock, with her hair tumbled like a gipsy's. The boys and girls waved and whistled to her from the cars, and a lad in silk bell-bottoms vaulted out of a driving seat and whirled her up in his arms, round and round. They were kissing—mouthing hungrily—when Natasha crossed the road and tried to slip in through the open gate without inviting comment. Amanda saw her, ducked away from the boy's open mouth, and grabbed at her sleeve.

"This is our Miss Collingwood," she told them all. Her eyes were very bright, and avoiding Natasha's. "Say hello to our Miss Collingwood, all of you!"

They chorused at her, whistled, and blew the car horns. The boy let go of Amanda's waist and slipped his hand round hers.

"Little Miss Collingwood, why don't you come with us to Positano, huh?" he said. He was heavily scented, and no boy: There was kohl round his pouchy eyes, and his Afro-styled hair was streaked with grey. "It's a party, Miss Collingwood, baby."

Natasha made herself limp and unresisting; willed herself not to scream into his face; even smiled.

"I'm not dressed for a party," she said. "But it's sweet of you to ask."

This brought a torrent of laughter and more blowing of car horns. Her tormentor flashed a white-toothed grin, and kissed her neck.

"Don't be uptight with me, Miss Collingwood, baby. Why you being uptight with me, huh?" He appealed to Amanda: "If this goddamned chick's the hired help, why don't you order her to come to Positano with us, Mandy-baby?"

Amanda smiled maliciously, then her expression changed. Eric had come to the gate, and was watching them shyly. Suddenly, Amanda had lost interest in the tormenting of Natasha.

"Stop making a fool of yourself, Bimbo," she said, "and let's go."

The man Bimbo released Natasha's wrist and patted her cheek. "A pity, baby. Pity," he said.

They were off with screaming tyres, horn-blasts, and shrieking; up the road, round the corner and away along the cliff road to the west.

Natasha went in, and the boy shut the gate.

"Better not lock it," he said. "Amanda's sure to be frightfully late back, and it only means that someone has to turn out and let her in." He smiled shyly. "Her chums are a rather eccentric and colourful lot, and not a bit your style, I should imagine."

"Or yours?" she asked.

He wrinkled his nose.

She had no immediate opportunity to tell Nathan Yardley about the small horror in the cemetery, and it seemed important to tell him—but not in front of a young boy, not so near his bedtime.

She had time to shower and change into a silk print; and they sat down to dinner in a long room in the older, lower part of the villa, with two sets of french windows opening out on to an iron balcony that seemed to hang over the sea. Daylight had retreated suddenly, and the gulf had filled with fishing boats, each with a friendly light on its stern.

Yardley sat at the other end of a refectory table opposite her, formal and distinguished-looking in white long-sleeved shirt and black knitted tie, with the candlelight doing interesting things with the very good planes of his face. Eric was between them, his back to the sea. The girl Giulietta had just served them with an iced soup.

"At present," said Yardley, "I'm sorting things out in my mind for the preparation of another book. It's a long and complex process. For me, it means the production of reams of indecipherable manuscript notes right out of the top of my head. Or, maybe, the whole thing's a piece of self-deception, and I'm really sitting back and enjoying the success of *Pride Goes Before*—and who could blame me, at my advanced age?"

"He really does work terribly hard," interposed Eric.

"Nothing that will involve Miss Collingwood at this stage," said Yardley, "though the correspondence will keep you busy enough, Miss Collingwood. And while we're about it, you'll be Natasha around here from now on. Or what do they call you for short?"

"My parents tried Sasha when I was young," she said. "But it never really caught on."

"Natasha it is then," said Yardley. "You'll eventually call me Nathan, of course, but I won't push you into it. Let it creep in when you feel right about it. More wine? Help Natasha to the carafe, old son."

Giulietta cleared the plates; and as she went out through the door, Natasha caught sight of another girl taking a quick peek at them.

"How many staff do you have?" she asked.

"The Capucci family," said Yardley. "Maria the cook is a widow. There are two daughters, Giulietta and Adriana. And old Mario, the grand-father, does the garden. They eat like vultures, but are absolutely honest; you'll not need to worry about locking up your valuables, or leaving money lying about."

The main course was cold lobster, delicately fresh, with a salad. And Nathan Yardley talked about his book. He did this—or so it seemed to Natasha—with the unself-conscious pride of an essentially simple and modest man who has discovered, quite late in his career, that he possesses an entirely unsuspected talent—and can hardly believe his good luck. She found herself warming to him.

"I tinkered around with the thing for five years," he said, "before it even occurred to me that it had the makings of a novel. It really began as a sort of diary, or a journal of my impressions. Then, gradually, I saw a shape coming. Next, I seemed to be seeing this shape in relationship to a set of characters—characters who sprang to life more or less ready-made."

"I think it's a marvellous book," said Natasha, sincerely, "and much more than a world-wide best seller. I really think it will live."

"That's the nicest thing you could have said, Natasha," said Nathan Yardley. With a sudden prickle of surprise, she saw that his eyes were brimming with tears of emotion. An instant later, he picked up his wine glass and hid them from her. She felt a warm wave of sympathy for him: a strong man, grown middle-aged and tired enough to value kindness. There were hidden riches of character, she told herself, that were well worth exploring in the owner of the Villa Gaspari.

"He's been swamped with all kinds of honours," said Eric. "A new university in West Africa has offered him the chair in

English, and he's had two honorary doctorates. Then he's been invited to America to accept a fabulous literary prize. I say, Nathan, did you remember to tell Susannah to write off and accept their . . . ?"

The boy stopped, and his young, unformed face reddened. Natasha looked down at her plate. There was a long silence.

"Bedtime, old chap," said Nathan Yardley presently. "Take some fruit with you, and don't forget to clean your teeth. And, for heaven's sake, don't wake us all up at the crack of dawn. He's rigged up a cricket net on the foreshore," he explained to Natasha, "and pressed one of the village boys into service as a demon bowler."

"Got to get into the first eleven next year," said Eric, picking himself a ripe peach from the dish. "I've set myself the target."

"Very commendable," said his step-father dryly, winking at Natasha. "I wish he'd have the same high aspirations about his Latin and mathematics!"

"Pig!" said Eric fondly, dropping a kiss on Yardley's forehead. "'Night, Nathan. 'Night, Natasha."

"Good night, Eric. See you in the morning."

Moments later, they heard him running, two at a time, up the steps, to a higher level of the villa. Nathan Yardley was pouring coffee.

"Let's take it out onto the balcony," he said.

The fishing boats had moved nearer; they could see the men's faces hovering over the stern lights, and the murmur of their voices came up out of the void, mingled with the sound of the sea moving through the great rocks. There was no light out on the balcony. Natasha sat in a wicker armchair; Yardley took a straight-backed seat by the french window, and the candlelight from the room played on his bowed profile.

"He's a nice boy, Eric," said Natasha. "And you have a very good relationship with him."

"Despite all legends to the contrary," he said, "I find the step-father relationship very productive, and at exactly the right remove for a good association with a young person. If Eric were my own flesh and blood, I might, for instance, find it difficult to accept that he's a mite priggish in his attitude to people who don't conform to his received norm. I was amused —but not one bit surprised—when he accepted you entirely without question. He's able to do this because your accent is good, your manners unexceptionable, and you dress well but unostentatiously. But, I can assure you, there's very much more to Eric than this. Poor Susannah possessed none of the social plusses I've mentioned, and yet—though he was, in consequence, that much less at ease with her—he was perfectly well able to like her."

Mention of the dead girl's name set Natasha to the task of assembling an opening phrase, to introduce the account of her violated grave. It seemed a very difficult thing to talk about.

"You gathered, though," continued Yardley, "that my step-daughter disliked Susannah. And I fancy the feeling was mutual. More coffee?"

"Thank you," said Natasha. "I went up to the cemetery this afternoon."

"It's a long way up," he said. "I wonder you weren't too tired after your flight."

"And I found the grave—her grave."

"We weren't able to do much in the time," he said. "And she had no relations, you see. But there will be a headstone when the local monumental mason gets around to it."

"Mr. Yardley," she blurted out desperately, "someone's torn her wreath to bits, and disfigured her photograph!"

The earthenware coffee jug shattered on the tiled floor of the balcony, and her leg was splattered with the hot liquid.

He groaned and got down on his knees with a handkerchief. She caught the scent of his cologne as their hands met at the level of her calf, and he withdrew his as if it had been burnt.

"Are you scalded badly?" he asked. "That was a damned clumsy thing to do."

"It's all right," she assured him.

He moved the broken shards into a corner with his foot. His face was in deep shadow.

"Torn, you said? And what was actually done to the photograph?"

She told him.

"What a vile trick."

"Yes."


Susannah Hislop, he told her, had been something of a treasure. How he would ever have managed finally to assemble his years of notes and disconnected fragments into the coherent whole of *Pride Goes Before* without her help was quite beyond imagining.

She had come to him as a temporary secretary, to handle his fan mail, just before the "Tell Me Another" show began to fade, and before he had seriously to face up to the prospect of working for a living, instead of receiving fat cheques for the ephemeral business of being a telly personality. A farm-bred girl from the west country, she was almost completely unread and uncultivated. But she was an accurate typist, a good speller (which he was not), and possessed a dogged appetite for slogging hard work.

With Susannah to drive him on, he told Natasha, the book was rounded off, polished, and away at the publisher before the last edition of "Tell Me Another" died in the night, and the final television cheque dropped on the mat. Looking deeply into his brandy glass in the half light of the dining room candles, he was able to admit that he owed more to Susannah Hislop than he could ever have repaid.

But, then, right out of the blue she had given her notice to quit. Why? Boredom. Picture a restless creature like Susannah, waiting for the long, slow gestation of another book like *Pride Goes Before*. There had already been two false starts; it could be another ten years. A bustling power-house like Susannah—a Thursday's child with a long way to go—just couldn't wait for that. In parenthesis, he hoped that Natasha wouldn't get bored; she fervently assured him that she wouldn't.

Later, after another brandy, he was able to add that Susannah had been a flawed character. Brought up, in a narrow and bigoted country way, by elderly parents, she had been quite unable to cope with the demands of her own passionate nature. Putting it in another way, he explained, poor Susannah's coming in headlong collision with the rampant southern Italian peasant male had been traumatic.

Had there been followers? Had there not! From Amalfi to Positano, from Maiori to Salerno; all of them hot-eyed, and most of them hopelessly too young for Susannah. There had been a lot of trouble: mutterings in the village café; and a few angry peasant mums shouting after Susannah in the street. At one stage, he had threatened to send her back to England on the next plane. Quite ridiculous.

And would that account for what had been done up in the cemetery? Well, it would go a long way towards explaining it. An affronted mother; jealous, perhaps, of what she might consider (though God knows on what evidence) to have been her son's lost virginity; or a susceptible youth whose tender manhood had been bruised by jilting. . . .

Now the fishing boats were standing far out into the gulf,

so that the lights were like fireflies and the voices muted. Natasha stirred in her seat.

"I think I'll say good night," she said.

"I hope this business hasn't worried you too much," he said. "It's quite absurd that you should be upset by it. But, believe me, it's all over now. What happened in the cemetery—what you saw—really doesn't have any significance."

He remained standing by the french window as she passed through the dining room, towards the door by which Eric had left. The table was cleared; it occurred to her that one of the women must have done it, very quietly, while Yardley had been speaking.

There was something else that had to be asked. Now—before she went up to her room: the room where Susannah Hislop had been a living person for the last time.

She opened the door and paused irresolutely, looking back at him. Their eyes met across the long room, above the wavering candle flames.

"It was an accident," he said quietly. "She didn't take her own life. First, because she had no reason to do such a thing; and second, because she was a very vital and positive sort of person, for whom self-destruction would have been so completely alien as to be completely beyond the compass of her imagining. She came out of the shower, her wet feet slipped on the tiles, and she fell over the low sill. The police were here, with their tape-measures and things, and were quite satisfied it was an accident. You'll find that we've had the sill raised with two extra courses of stonework. That's it. That's all of it, Natasha."

"Thank you," she said. "Good night."

"Good night. Don't worry."

Don't worry. A few minutes later, she was standing in the death chamber, by the window. There were two layers of new stone, bringing the level of the sill to the height of her waist, freshly whitewashed on the inside.

The stars were out, and spent wavelets were hissing in the shingle. Perched on the corners of the flat roof of the building where she had dined, two of the statues that kept vigil over the Villa Gaspari gesticulated out across the gulf. Down in the village, someone was thrumming a guitar.

Don't worry.

She screwed up her nerve ends, she strained her eyes to peer down into the kitchen courtyard, but it was too dark to see if the old man had managed to work away the bloodstain.

In her dream, the thing came out of the cemetery and glided barefoot down the steps in the moonlight. Knowing that it was a dream, and that she was going to be trapped in a horror of her own imagining, she tried to wake up—but failed. And now the thing was much nearer.

The iron gates of the Villa Gaspari groaned open to the touch of a cold hand, and the thing was soon at her door. There was only one way to shock herself to wakefulness, but the concept of it was scarcely less dreadful than that of staying to face a dream-image of the walking dead; nevertheless she clutched it to her as a last resort, and concentrated on keeping the indigo blue rectangle of the open window imprinted in her mind. Escape lay that way.

She was not prepared for the sudden shift in the intensity of her panic once the thing was inside the room with her. When it was standing inside the door, and when it was beginning to move towards her—soiled with earth, broken-necked, and reeking—she lived through a spasm of horror of such rapid increase as—mercifully—to pass beyond the limit of her mind's apprehension, leaving a void that was quickly taken over by the raw impulse to escape.

The distance from the bed to the window was sometimes a quicksand that sucked at her running feet, sometimes a moving escalator that left her standing still. But when the hands of the dead Susannah Hislop touched her, she was able to will her arms to telescope out and, grasping the sill, pull herself forward and dive headlong into the darkness.

The impact woke her up, palpitating, and slimy with her own sweat. She took off her sodden nightdress and, slipping on a towelling robe, went out into the dawn.

The wind was blowing in from the sea, swaying the tips of the cypresses and causing the long waves to curl over and break against the rocks below the villa. The sky was the colour of smoked mother-of-pearl, like the light from an old horn lantern.

She walked down two flights of steps, till she was standing by an oleander shrub that overhung the wall. Below her was the lowest level of the villa, with the gesticulating statues, the narrow beach, the hissing waves.

And someone was down there. . . .

It was Amanda. She was still wearing the long frock of the previous night. She was leaning against a rough stone wall at the top of the beach, arms folded against her breast, chin in hand, and staring out to sea.

## 4

There was no question of trying to sleep again; not with the dream-image of dead Susannah Hislop so near at hand and perhaps within calling distance. Natasha went back to her room and filled out the rest of the dawn hour by writing a letter to Veronica, the girl with whom she had lately shared a flat in St. John's Wood; but it ended—shorn of any reference to Susannah's death and the circumstances surrounding it—by bearing such slight relevance to the sum of her experiences at the Villa Gaspari that she tore it up. By that time, there were pots clattering in the kitchen quarters below her window. She wondered if Amanda had come up from the shore.

She put on an off-white linen trouser suit and a lot of mascara. Down at the oleander shrub, she was able to check that Amanda was no longer on the beach. It was quite different in the sunshine. The cypresses were still and dark against the blueness, and the sea was calm.

"Put a bit of pudding behind it, Guido! That's better." This was followed by the sharp snick of wood on leather.

Craning over the wall, she saw Eric in white shirt and slacks held up with a multi-coloured necktie. He was standing at one end of a strip of coconut matting near the top of the beach, cricket bat at the ready. Another boy—older, Italian, barefoot, and naked save for a pair of skimpy shorts—bowled the ball at him down a tunnel of netting. Again, snick—and Eric sent it slamming against the netting.

The bowler saw Natasha above him and preened himself self-consciously, arching his bronzed chest and showing a lot of very white teeth. Eric followed his companion's gaze and raised his bat in salutation.

"'Morning, Miss Collingwood. Hope we didn't wake you up."

"I was already up," she said.

Eric nodded, and took stance again with great seriousness.

"Give me one with plenty of length, Guido!" Guido gave Natasha a regretful glance and went back to work.

The smell of coffee led her to the room where they had dined the previous evening. The table was laid for four, and Giulietta appeared within a minute, elbowing her way in through the kitchen door with a tray of coffee and bread rolls.

Natasha wished her good morning and the girl nodded. There were dark circles under her eyes. Giulietta had been crying again.

Natasha breakfasted alone. All through it, the click of bat on ball came up from the shore. Nathan Yardley did not put in an appearance, but she met him afterwards, coming down the steps from the upper level. There were two men behind him—one of them in uniform.

"Er—Natasha, there's been a little trouble . . ." Her employer gestured towards his companions. "The police—that's to say, the inspector here—would like a few words with you."

"Good morning, Miss Collingwood. I am Inspector Pinturicchio and that is rather a mouthful, isn't it? I'm sorry to trouble you. Can we have a quiet word together?" He gestured towards a low wall that lay in the shadow of the building, and the manner in which he turned his back upon Nathan Yardley was pointedly dismissive.

They sat together on the wall, half facing each other. Pinturicchio was stocky, thick-set, and thirtyish, dressed as if for a holiday, in a floral shirt that was nipped in at the waist, and unbuttoned at neck and cuff to show plenty of his black-pelted muscle tissue. His southern eyes were predatory, humorous, and peasant-shrewd. He spoke English with scarcely any accent.

"It's about the girl who died here," he said. "Someone has been doing bad things to her grave."

"I know," said Natasha. "I walked up there yesterday afternoon and saw it."

Pinturicchio nodded. "More has been done overnight," he said. "And when I came to inform Mr. Yardley, he told me what you had already witnessed." He picked up a pebble and flipped it, finger and thumb, over the wall. "I wonder, Miss Collingwood—if it wouldn't upset you too much—if you would be so kind as to accompany me up to the cemetery and show me exactly what damage had been done when you were up there yesterday afternoon at—what time did you say?"

"It—must have been just after seven-fifteen," she said. "I saw the grave had been spoilt when I went back through the cemetery, though it was untouched when I first went in."

"And when was that?" he asked.

"I climbed up to the plateau above, lay down there, and dozed off," she said. "I was asleep for about an hour."

"Between about six-fifteen and seven-fifteen—that was when the grave was disturbed, then?"

"Yes."

"Shall we go, then?" He got up and looked across at Nathan Yardley, who stood with the uniformed policeman near the entrance to the long dining room. "There'll be no need for you to come, sir," he grinned. "Miss Collingwood will be in good hands."

And what's more, thought Natasha, for two pins he'd pinch my bottom.

There was another uniformed policeman guarding the cemetery gates from a small group of wide-eyed children; he saluted Pinturicchio and let them both in. The clamour of the cicadas was loud in the walled enclosure; so was the clash of a shovel against earth and rock. Two men in workmen's overalls were over by Susannah Hislop's grave. Natasha was shocked to see that one of them was waist deep and wielding the shovel. She paused—but the inspector took her elbow reassuringly.

"There is nothing bad to see," he said. "And it will soon be completely filled in again."

The workmen were sun-dried little old men, and they greeted the inspector familiarly by his first name—Aldo. The one in the grave wiped the sweat from his face and muttered some wry comment, to which Pinturicchio made a sharp reply, with a swift glance towards Natasha.

"Was—was she . . . ?" began Natasha, appalled.

"The coffin was not disturbed," said Pinturicchio quickly. "Though that was probably the intention. But the intruder was not aware of the size of the task he'd set himself. You see, in this cemetery they have to dig out a lot of rock when they make the graves, and it is all put back when the hole is filled up." He gestured towards some sizeable pieces of rock that lay in the pile of earth at the edge of the hole. "It seems possible that the intruder was not able to finish his task before the cemetery sweeper came to work just after six o'clock and disturbed him."

"But, why? Why would anyone do such a thing?"

The little old men were regarding her from under their dark berets. Pinturicchio spread his hands and hunched his broad shoulders.

"You tell me, Miss Collingwood. It is beyond my comprehension. So let us take it by easy stages. What had been done here when you came down from the plateau yesterday afternoon at about seven-fifteen?"

She told him. The trampled lilies were still scattered among the earth that was now strewn on the path. At the mention of the violated photograph, Pinturicchio set the man with the shovel on to scraping up the edges of the pile. Presently, he uncovered the plastic holder with the picture still in place.

Pinturicchio stared down at it for a while.

"What manner of woman was she," he said, "to have generated so much hatred as this?"

The man had put aside his shovel; together with his companion, he was selecting the largest of the stones and laying them in the shallow hole. She noticed that there was a pile of concrete building blocks nearby, and materials to make mortar.

Pinturicchio was looking at her; had been looking at her for quite a few seconds.

"How long had you known the late Miss Hislop?"

She thought that she had misheard the question; it was several moments before she registered that he had really said it; at the end of that time, his glance had become less searching, and he was smiling at her.

"You startled me," she said. "Hadn't you been told that I only came yesterday—and that I'd never met Susannah Hislop?"

He only nodded and scratched his ear. She was left with the feeling that something had remained unresolved.

One of the workmen was mixing sand and cement when they left. The poor remains of Susannah Hislop were to be afforded more substantial protection than broken rock and loose earth.

But—protection from whom?

She parted from Pinturicchio outside the villa. He drove off towards Amalfi in a police car, and waved to her before it turned the first corner.

She met Nathan Yardley coming up the steps from the dining room carrying a cup of coffee. His face was lined with anxiety.

"Was it very bad?" he asked. "The inspector told me more or less what had happened. The vandals didn't get to the coffin?"

"No."

"It really is terrible," he said. "I don't know what to begin to think. Best thing is to put it out of our minds, I suppose. Do you feel equal to doing a little work? I think it would be a good idea if I showed you the ropes."

"Yes, I'd like that," she said.

The room he called the office was on the same level as her bedroom. It had limewashed walls, a stone floor, and a very busy electric fan that looked this way and that. A modern steel desk, chair, and filing cabinet made up the furniture.

Yardley showed her where to find the stationery, and opened a folder that lay on the desk beside the telephone.

"This is the fan mail," he said. "It finds its way here by diverse routes: some via publishers all over the world, some from my agent, and then there's the occasional enterprising reader who actually manages to get hold of this address."

"And you reply to it all? There seems an awful lot."

"Susannah," he said. "Susannah worked out a very good system. In this drawer, you'll find three stock letters of general thanks that fit most situations. They're all hand-typed, and all you have to do is put dear so-and-so at the top. Actually, you will find that you'll be able to forge my signature quite adequately after a while. And in this drawer is a supply of photographs, all autographed. You only send these on request."

"And what about the letters that aren't covered by one of the stock replies?" she asked.

"You stick those back in the folder and we have a blitz on them one morning a week. All right?"

Natasha nodded. Yardley crossed over to the door. "I'm driving down to Amalfi," he said. "Back in time for a drink on the terrace before lunch. See you then."

Surprisingly, the daunting wad of letters in the fan mail folder took her less than an hour to deal with; the modest elegancies of the three stock letters of reply (surely drafted by Nathan Yardley, and not by the almost illiterate Susannah) were more than adequate answer to the rubbishy stuff that was sent to the author of what was currently the world's favourite book.

The small diversions of the office occupied her for another ten minutes. After that, there was the view from the window, which was the left eye to the right eye of her own bedroom window: the wide sweep of the gulf, and the breakers among the rocks below; but instead of the kitchen yard (and the rusty patch of dried blood), it looked down on a small terrace, where Amanda and Eric were lounging in deck chairs; they were slack-limbed and bronzed in the white sunlight, with unread paperbacks, empty coffee cups and jazzily coloured towels strewn about them. The murmur of their conversation was carried up to her from time to time: a bumble-bumble on the still air.

At about half-past eleven, she decided to quit playing at work for the morning, and walk down to see what the village had to offer in the way of shops.

Although her father had been only an impoverished Suffolk squire, with scarcely the means to repair the roof of his lovely tumbledown manor house, dredge his moat, or clear the weeds from his stew-pond, Natasha, through the good graces of her mother's people—who were not only richly well-connected in England, but also on the Continent—had travelled widely, especially in Italy, from an early age. She was able, quite easily, to accept the elements—visual, tactile, and odoriferous—that make up the average southern Italian village.

The village near the Villa Gaspari—on that morning in early spring—looked like a picture postcard, felt dry and sandy to the touch, and smelt faintly of decayed fish and urine.

Without descending all the way, she could see that the last flourish of the winding coast road ended in a hollow square of limewashed buildings below her. There was a café in the square, where two men in black were hunched at an outside table. Many-coloured fishing boats were drawn up on the crescent-shaped beach, their lacy nets suspended to dry. The clear air played tricks with the perspective, diminishing distance, so that it seemed to her that she need only reach out her hand to touch the worn flagstones of the square, and only stretch a little farther to explore the textured wall of the old fort that stood sentinel on the far side of the small bay.

Steps led down through a rabbit warren of tall buildings, offering an intriguing short cut to the square. Before she had gone more than a little way down, the high walls had risen all around her, shutting out everything but an irregular shape of cerulean sky, and bathing her in chill shadows. The café in the square and the fort on the far hill, which had seemed so near, were in another world; and she was hemmed in by flaking walls and windows like blind eyes. There was no sign of anyone, but when the steps brought her round a corner, she heard the laughter of children from somewhere ahead. It was not the laughter of gay innocence; there was mockery and menace there.

The quality of the laughter primed her unease, so that she

nearly turned back; but another bend brought the children into sight below her.

Natasha registered about six or eight of them—urchin boys in faded and ragged shirts and shorts, barefoot. They were playing with—tormenting—a kitten. Laughing and chanting, they were tossing the writhing scrap of white fur from one to the other, like a handball. Sooner or later, it had to fall and be injured—this was clearly a concomitant of the game; the throwing and the catching were loose and haphazard, and a fumbling catch brought fresh shrieks of mockery.

"Stop it!"

The echo of her shout, reflected back from the enclosing walls, seemed unnaturally loud, and some arcane prompting made her repeat the words in a harsh whisper, this time in Italian.

"You detestable creatures. How can you be so cruel?" she hissed at them, for good measure.

The one who was holding the kitten—he was bigger and taller than most of the others, and there were the beginnings of a moustache on his upper lip, though he could scarcely have been more than eleven—backed away from her, wide-eyed with alarm, as she approached him, hands extended.

"Give that poor little thing to me!" she demanded.

It could have ended there. Receiving no support from his silent and overawed companions, the boy was on the point of obeying her—when the toe of her sandal caught on the edge of a flagstone, and she sprawled forward onto her knees. Her handbag fell, burst open, and sprayed money, lipstick, powder compact, a bottle of aspirin, and bits and bobs over a wide area.

Her brief domination was instantly washed out. Hooting with unholy joy, the children went among her belongings, kicking at them with their bare toes; she saw her powder compact skitter out of sight down the next flight of steps. Her right leg was doubled underneath her; when she rose and straightened it up, the heel of her sandal caught in the hem of her skirt, and the material ripped. They saw it, and squealed the louder.

Blinded, now, with tears of anger, she went for the boy with the kitten; but he was playing with her now, ducking and weaving like a boxer, and goading her on. She made a wild grab for the little animal—but he tossed it over her head, where it was caught by one of his companions.

And so it went. Now it was a nightmare game of volley-ball, with the sobbing, half-hysterical girl making short rushes from one to another of her tormentors, to rescue the kitten. Her every attempt only increased the hazard to the small creature; it was squealing continuously with terror.

Finally, she closed with a child who was slower and smaller than the rest; and she was wresting the kitten from his hands, when the rest of them intervened. They were all about her. One of them was kneeling and pulling at her ankle, to overbalance her. Her hair was in her eyes, so that she could see nothing. Now they were pawing at her from all sides. When she felt small hands kneading her breasts, she began to scream.

Quite suddenly, they fell apart from her and were sullenly silent. Brushing the hair from her eyes, she saw a taller figure dominating the group, and recognised the newcomer as Guido, the youth who had been bowling at the cricket net that morning. He had her first tormentor—the big child with the incipient moustache—by the collar of his ragged shirt, and was quietly growling at him, menacingly, face-to-face. Their counterpoised profiles were almost identical: darkly Phoenician. They were quite obviously brothers.

Guido ended whatever he had to say with a surprisingly brutal slap to the side of the other's head that jerked him back and set him crying: He raced off up the steps and ducked into a dark doorway. The other children drifted away in twos and threes, their large eyes lingering expressionlessly on Natasha.

Guido scooped up the kitten, who had so far recovered from its ordeal as to be happily playing with the flap of her fallen handbag. He handed her kitten and handbag together.

"They are bad boys. Do very bad things," he said, in English.

"Thank you," said Natasha.

He made a lot of play with his teeth, of which he was obviously inordinately proud, and with good reason: He was moist-mouthed, and he was constantly licking his teeth dry with a very pink and healthy-looking tongue. Physical—the word sprang immediately to her mind, like an advertising slogan; Guido was aggressively and unashamedly physical, from his brown, bare feet to the crown of his sleek, dark head.

He picked up the rest of her fallen belongings and slipped them into her open bag while she held it. The kitten writhed in her grasp and made a tentative dab at his finger, tiny claws unsheathed.

"He doesn't seem any the worse for wear," said Natasha, registering the fact that Guido was making a *longeur* of the business with her bag. "Well, I'll be on my way," she added briskly. "Thanks awfully for your help."

She nodded brightly to him, and continued on down the steps in the direction of the square (and how long ago it seemed since she resolved to take the short cut down to it), still carrying the kitten. She was obviously stuck with the little thing; it was out of the question to leave it at the mercy of those dreadful young louts.

Guido was still with her, descending the steps beside her, bare feet padding dryly. She wondered how much farther it was to the bottom, where there were people and sunlight.

"How you like Italy, then?" he asked.

"Very much," she said. "I spent a lot of time here when I was a child," she added, flatly.

"You like Italians?"

The steps bent round another tall tenement block, and there seemed no end in sight.

"Yes," she said.

He laughed. "You wanna like Italian men," he said, "'cos they making good lovers. Very strong."

And—lest she should think that he didn't know about English girls being push-overs—he made a quick follow-up by slipping his arm round her waist. Kitten in one arm and handbag in the other, there was little else she could do but try to side-step away from him. His grip tightened, and he brought his other arm into play, turning her to face him. He kissed her, and there didn't seem any point in being coy and maidenly, or doing something silly like bringing her forehead down on the bridge of his nose. It was a kiss of surprising tenderness, and his breath carried garlic. She resolutely kept her mouth closed against his probing tongue. It struck her that he probably wasn't a day over sixteen.

"Right," she said, stepping back from him when his grip slackened. "We'll call that payment for getting me out of an embarrassing situation. But don't pester me again, young man."

He looked genuinely astonished, and verging on anger.

"You don't want love?" he demanded.

"I would suggest a little time at the cricket net," she said firmly, and with good humour. "And, after that, a cold shower."

She ran down the steps, not waiting to see the effect of her snub, which she had delivered to him in Italian. As she turned the last corner, and saw the splash of sunlight on the worn flagstones of the square below, he shouted something after her in his own language.

She was still reconstituting the sounds into phrases when

she walked out across the square, and past the café tables, where the two men in black were still bowed over their empty glasses. They did not look up when her shadow fell across them.

As the phrases took firm shape, she felt a curious prickling of her skin.

What Guido's angry retort had amounted to, give or take a sound or two that might slightly have changed the shape of the meaning—and minus the obscenities—was this:

*"You are a whore and a tease, like the other one. And you'll end up being thrown out of the window, like her!"*

## 5

She bought safety pins at a spotless chemist's shop beyond the square: The white-coated, goatee-bearded old man behind the counter consented to hold the kitten, and turned aside with grave politeness while she pinned up the ripped hem of her skirt. She also bought a new lipstick, aspirins, and some suntan lotion. The chemist rushed round to open the door for her, and bowed her out.

The café in the square was too uncomfortably near to the area of the tenements and the street of winding steps: No telling if the obscene urchins wouldn't be watching her with their dirty, holy innocents' eyes. There was another small café close by the chemist's. She took an outside seat under a red-white-and-green-striped umbrella, and ordered coffee from a pale girl in mauve.

". . . *you'll end up being thrown out of the window, like her!*"

Natasha tried out the sentence several times, in Italian, but it always ended up the same way. The operative verb had distinctly been *gettato* and not *cadendo*.

Stacked up against what Nathan Yardley had told her about the tragedy, it didn't add up to much in the way of evidence. Nathan had been quite specific, in his assurances to her, about the accident angle: the wet feet from the shower, slipping on the tiles; the sill that was raised up, to prevent such a thing from ever happening again. The boy Guido's horrific statement, she told herself, was no more than a wild riposte to her squashing snub: a barbed thrust from a young Latin male scorned, as direct and uncalculated as the strike and bite of a disturbed adder. As to the content of his thrust—that Susannah had been deliberately pushed from the window—this was the kind of loose gossip that took root in small communities the world over, and was by no means restricted to the villages of the Salerno peninsula. She recalled how, in her own native hamlet in West Suffolk, it was still firmly held that the late rector (a cleric of transparently virtuous appetites) had not only been a secret drunkard, but had been responsible for all the unexplained local pregnancies from the middle nineteen-fifties till his death at the age of eighty.

Gravely regarding the kitten (who was ravenously lapping milk from her saucer, under the table), Natasha assured herself that Guido had merely snatched at a handy piece of local scurrility to throw at her.

She was relating this to the violating of Susannah's grave, when a remarkable figure sailed close by her table, continued a further half-dozen steps, paused, and turned to peer at her through—of all things—a lorgnette.

"Ah, you must be the new child of whom we have heard." She was an Italian lady of advanced but indeterminate years, dressed entirely in black, in toque bonnet, shoulder-length cape, and ankle-length skirt—in defiance of the midday heat. She spoke good English in a richly textured contralto.

The apparition came upon her again, and, amid the odour of face powder and patchouli, Natasha meekly submitted to having her chin taken between plump, gloved fingers that turned her head from side to side, to meet the detailed examination from the short-sighted old eyes behind the lorgnette.

"What a pretty child. You must come and have tea with me tomorrow. Come at five. What is your name, my dear?"

"Natasha Collingwood, ma'am."

"Natasha is a pretty name. I knew several persons of that name, in Russia, you know, where I visited frequently when I was a young girl. I travelled with my father, by train. It took a very long time. Do you know Russia well? The air of Petrograd is very fine." She opened a jet reticule and produced a paper bag, which she held out to Natasha. "Have one, my dear. No? I am quite addicted." She popped a large, violet-tinted sugared almond in her mouth and crushed it between a near-perfect set of teeth. Everything about her, Natasha decided, was a curious blending of age and youth: The face, though thickly ladened with powder, was plump and unlined; yet the skin of the neck hung from the jawline in wattles. The eyes, though pitifully myopic, were as bright, black, and lively as an old falcon's.

"I must leave you now, my dear," she said. "I am having my likeness painted, and the artist is coming for a sitting at twelve. Until tomorrow at five. *Au revoir.*"

"But . . . I don't know where you live," faltered Natasha.

"Everyone," said her new friend, "everyone in Italy knows where I live." And, with that, she walked away across the street, in and out of the sunlight and the shadow, till her sable form turned the corner and went from sight.

Natasha quizzed the pale girl in mauve, when she paid for the coffee. She only had to mention the elderly lady dressed all in black.

"Ah," said the girl in tones of great reverence. "That is the *principessa*. The Principessa Adelina Josefa, who lives in the big palazzo on the hill above the church." And she pointed away across the pantiled rooftops to where, at the inland edge of the village, the upper part of a Baroque portico rose above a crumbling basilica.

The girl tapped her forehead with her fingertip. "The *principessa* is a little—well—you know what I mean, *signorina*."

It was out of the question to return to the Villa Gaspari by way of the street of steps; instead, she took the coast road out of the square, and found it, in fact, to be much quicker.

The outer walls of the villa came in sight round the bend, and there was a red sports car parked close by the gate. As she drew closer, she saw that the windscreen was cracked and crazed, and the front fender bashed in. The cream leather upholstery of the driver's seat was splattered with fresh blood that was beginning to darken and dry in the hot sun.

The gate creaked open to her touch. She saw a trail of dripped blood all the way across the terrace and down the steps. She ran. The kitten protested and started to scrabble in her arms, so she put it inside her room and shut the door.

She met Amanda coming towards her up the next flight of steps; the girl looked amused.

"What's happened?"

"Nathan doing his Grand Prix act again," replied Amanda. "Bashed into a truck on one of the bends from Amalfi. Don't ever take a ride with him—not if you can dream up a good alibi—or you'll have your face through the windscreen."

"Is he hurt badly?"

Amanda's smile, on closer inspection, was entirely without good humour; her lower lip was slack and out of control, and her eyes were shifty. She turned her face away, as if conscious that she was displaying too much emotion.

"I'm not a damn doctor!" she snapped, and ran on up the steps.

Nathan Yardley's room was in the lower building, above the dining room: Natasha found her way there by following the blood trail—and the sound of excited Italian voices. The

Capuccis were grouped by the open door; their chattering died as they saw her, and they moved aside to let her pass.

Yardley lay on a blood-dappled white counterpane, on an iron bed in a large and plainly furnished room. A small man who had to be a doctor was winding a bandage round his right knee. Yardley was holding a cloth to his forehead, and wincing with agony at every turn of the bandage. Eric stood by the window, white-faced—looking as if he might be sick any moment.

"Can I help?" asked Natasha.

"Is coming on all right, *signorina*," said the little doctor, who flashed her a sudden, eager smile. "The morphia will do the trick in a couple of ticks."

Yardley opened one eye and groaned.

"What an awful thing to happen," said Natasha. She took the cloth from his forehead and re-folded it at a clean piece. There was a darkening bruise reaching from the hairline down the right side of the face as far as the jaw; the blood was coming from his nose.

"He says I've got to go to hospital for a check-up," said Yardley.

"Quite essential," said the doctor, cheerfully. "We must assure ourselves that there is no concussion. Then there is the patella—which is to say the kneecap, you know—which may be cracked. Impact with the dashboard, you see. If it is fractured, it will have to be removed. There is no other way. I have telephoned the hospital in Naples, and they are sending out an ambulance."

"Is it going to be a long job?" asked Yardley.

The doctor tied the end of the knee bandage in a butterfly bow and straightened up. It was only then that Natasha saw that he was a hunchback. He bowed to her, and slid his amused gaze to the man on the bed.

"If the X-rays are negative, you could be back here by, say, tomorrow evening, *signor*," he said. "Leaving aside the question of serious concussion, which seems to me to be contra-indicated, there is the matter of the patella. If you have to have it removed, you will be able to walk on crutches in three months' time. In six months you will walk with a limp. Ten years from now, when the weather is maybe a little chilly, you will also walk with a limp. Cracking the patella is not a big joke. It will teach you not to play Tazio Nuvolari in your little Alfa-Romeo." He turned to Natasha again. "I don't know—they weren't able to tell me—when the ambulance will come, but it will be some time this afternoon. Till then, he should just rest as quietly as possible. He has had a dose of morphia to deaden the pain in the knee, and he should sleep."

"I feel pretty drowsy now," said Yardley. "Thank God this nose-bleed's stopped."

"That was the worst part, for me," said Eric. "Seeing them carry you in with blood streaming from your face. I thought . . ."

With a stab of compassion, Natasha saw that the boy was near to tears. And that wouldn't do, she told herself. Not in front of a woman, not to mention an Italian—not for an aspirant of the first cricket eleven.

"Eric, dear," she said, taking his arm and leading him towards the door of what seemed to be Yardley's dressing room, "be a pet and make yourself useful. You probably know where Nathan keeps his toilet gear and bits and pieces. Pack him an overnight bag to take in the ambulance, would you?"

The boy blinked vigorously and flashed her a glance of adoring gratitude. "Sure. I'll do it right away, Natasha. I'll put in handkerchiefs and things. Do you suppose they'll provide pyjamas at the hospital?"

"Perhaps," she said. "But they'll be rather dreary and institutional. Pack him a couple of pairs of something gay."

"Nothing too sexy," cracked Yardley. "Not with those hot-eyed Neopolitan nurses."

They all laughed, and the doctor picked up his bag.

"So nice to meet you, *signorina,*" he said. "It's plain to see that I'm leaving Signor Yardley in tip-top hands till the ambulance arrives."

She gave him her hand. "Thank you, doctor."

"If any snags, just give me a tinkle down in the village. All you do is lift the receiver and ask the operator for Dr. Negretti. *Arriverderci, signorina.*" He left.

The bed creaked as Yardley made a half-hearted attempt to turn over on his side, and gave up with a moan of pain.

"Would you like me to read to you, till you drop off?" she said.

He nodded without opening his eyes. "Mmmm. Anything, so long as it isn't *Pride Goes Before!*"

The sun had dipped behind the high hills, which were all in purple shadow. A sudden wind was blowing a slight spindrift from the wave tops, and her bare arms goosefleshed at its touch. The beach was empty. It occurred to her that she was standing in the same spot where she had seen Amanda standing in the early morning: another girl looking out to sea.

The ambulance from Naples, in the event, had not arrived till nearly six o'clock, by which time she had come to know Nathan Yardley a whole lot better. And, perhaps, he understood her better, too. She hoped so.

Natasha counted the incoming waves, and let her mind drift back, languorously, over the long afternoon. . . .

Despite the morphia, Yardley had not slept. She read aloud to him from the continental edition of the *Courier,* including the woman's page and the property news. The sports pages made him thrash around and moan with pain.

*"Oh, for heaven's sake, talk to me, Natasha. Tell me about yourself."*

What to tell? She dabbed the sweat from his brow, and started in on a brief life. There was childhood, and that was all about not being as rich as all one's friends, so that Daddy drank too much when quarter days came around, at which time also, Mummy went about with her eyes red-rimmed from crying in private corners where the children shouldn't see her. Childhood, also, was lovely things like ponies and hay-making, carol-singing and butterscotch; and for her—Natasha —it was also writing long and swaggering historical romances, in careful roundhand, that sometimes covered as many as three feint-ruled exercise books, which she read aloud, one chapter a day, to her siblings, Joe, Marie, and Jess.

Had her ambition been to be a writer, then?—an interruption from Nathan Yardley. And, shyly, she told him yes. That was why she had worked so desperately hard for a scholarship to university. The outcome of three years at London had been a first-class honours degree, plus a collection of short stories and a novella that must surely have been thumbed by every publisher's reader in the business. After that, it was a straight choice between teaching and secretarial work—and she had plumped for the latter. End of brief life.

Yardley didn't know about painters, he told her, because he'd never been able to get round the National Gallery without succumbing to an attack of the yawns; and a tin ear made him incompetent to make a value judgement on the art of the musician. But us writers have got to stick together, he said, because there's only going to be us left to tell them all about truth and love and walking upright when this world finally collapses beneath the weight of uncaring. She recognized the paraphrase of a speech by the hero of *Pride Goes Before,* and the sincerity of his delivery hit her like a shock wave. Her heart gave a treacherous lurch when he turned his head aside to hide his tears.

After that, he wanted to hear her read some of her stuff. She went upstairs to fetch it from her room (the white kitten darted out at her from under the bed, and they played tag for a short while) and carried down the thick folder full of scuffed typescript with the rusting paper clips. What did he want to hear? A passage from the novella, or one of the short stories? He asked for some of the stories. She turned to her favourite and began reading.

For all that he was on his bed of pain, and lathered with sweat, Nathan Yardley was a good listener. He did it with his eyes shut, and his expressive face reacted to every nuance, the way a good theatre audience reacts on a good night. He nodded, grunted, grinned, did all the right things. Greatly encouraged, she read well, and the stories—even those passages that had once seemed to go limpingly, and that she had long promised herself to rewrite—came across better than she would have believed after—how long was it?—four years.

His judgement was at once brutal and beautiful. Some of it was pretty crude stuff, he told her; but don't let anyone—not all the publishers in the world—ever convince her that she was anything other than a writer. A born writer. A natural.

Then it was Natasha's turn to cry, and he gave her his handkerchief to blow into, reached up and patted her shoulder, as well as he was able, and promised to commend her work to his own publishers just as soon as he got back from the hospital. She was still choking back tears of pure happiness when she stood with the others at the gates of the villa, to see him off in the ambulance at six o'clock, conscious of a very special bond between her and the man who was being whisked away to his expensive private room in the hospital at Naples, over the hillcrest and forty kilometres as the crow flies, for his check-up on the morrow.

It grew darker, and the lights were coming on in the windows of the houses round the bay. Her mood of euphoria had dissipated, leaving her with a sense of depression and slight apprehension. Here goes a day that began with a nightmare, escalated into real horror, and ended with something wonderful.

She went back to the horror: She took out the words of the boy Guido, and strung them up in front of her mind's eye: ". . . *you'll end up being thrown out of the window, like her.*"

Some people—her friend and flatmate Veronica for one—would have left this job at a moment's notice and be flying back to London tonight, on receipt of such a threat. She tried to picture poor Veronica, who suffered from nervous asthma, trying to explain to Nathan Yardley the reason for her leaving. It was a far-fetched conceit that made Natasha smile, and her mood lightened.

The shadows of the mountains were moving across the sea, as she turned to go back up to the villa. Now Nathan's away, she thought, I suppose I'm nominal chatelaine of the Villa Gaspari, which means I have to look after a rather nice schoolboy and a rather nasty teen-aged girl. And I wonder what's for dinner tonight?

Passing the kitchen block, she smelt garlic and fish, and heard the womenfolk chattering excitedly. Quenching an impulse to go in and play the chatelaine, she went up to her room, with a shower and a change into something both warmer and more formal in mind.

The room had retained the sun's warmth, so there was no need to close the windows against the chill air of the new night. She unzipped her dress and slid open the wardrobe and riffled through the hangers to get an inspiration about what to wear for the rest of what had been an extremely fraught day.

Then she realised that something was missing: the kitten.

She laughed to herself for forgetting the white kitten. The little scrap had been shut up for hours, and heaven knows how hungry and thirsty it must be by now, or how many messes it had made here or in the bathroom.

She called the white kitten: "Kitty, kitty . . ."

It wasn't in the bathroom, either.

There was no good reason for her to have looked out of the window: She certainly made no conscious association with the missing kitten and the death of Susannah Hislop.

The kitchen courtyard was deeply shadowed by its encompassing walls, darkening the stone with which it was paved, but this only served to show up, in more startling contrast, the little white shape that lay in the centre of a carmine star.

The white kitten had died on the very spot that old Mario the gardener had worked so hard to make clean.

Dinner was a disaster. For a start, the Capuccis had been affronted by her bursting in through the kitchen and into the yard, to gather up the dead kitten. The old man had taken it from her and had buried it under a lemon tree on one of the garden terraces; but Giuliana's averted eyes were still sullen when she stooped to offer Natasha the dish of grilled trout with almonds.

"You must realise that they don't subscribe to English attitudes," drawled Amanda. Amanda, surprisingly *soignée* in a midnight blue long dress, had filled her wine glass three times and was enjoying the situation. "They're entirely realistic and unsentimental about animals that don't earn their keep—and there are about ten cats per mouse in this neck of the woods, so the feline population is somewhat under-employed in the Salerno peninsula. Add to that, you *did* act as if you were practically accusing them of chucking the creature out of the window."

"I was dreadfully upset," said Natasha. "It was my fault, leaving him in the room with the window open."

"We all heard you being upset," said Amanda, dryly. "As they must all have heard you, as far away as Capri."

"Well, I think we should change the subject," said Eric. "For Natasha's sake."

His sister turned her head slowly towards him. Speaking very deliberately, she said: "I think you should get on and eat your dinner, little boy. And when you've done that, you can ask to leave the table. Then you can go up to bed, where, under the warm, smelly darkness of the sheets, you can indulge yourself with thoughts of the first cricket eleven, and other masturbation fantasies."

Eric burst into tears. Dinner was certainly a disaster.

## 6

Eric had entirely recovered his spirits by breakfast time, which spoke well for his powers of snapping back. He had been down at the cricket net since an early hour—Natasha had heard the sound of bat on ball—and last night's weepy boy might never have been. She wondered if Guido had told him about their encounter in the village.

"There's a sort of religious festival tomorrow evening," Eric said, thickly plastering marmalade on toast, "and I'll take you there if you like, Natasha. It isn't far to walk. Just up the hill and along a bit. There's a procession, and it's all rather spooky. Like to come?"

"I'd love to. Thanks, Eric." They were alone. Amanda, who had called for a second litre of wine at dinner, was still in bed and probably regretting it.

"We should have news about Nathan this morning," said Eric.

"If we don't hear by midday, I'll ring the hospital," she said.

Eric gulped down the last of his coffee and left, telling her that he had loads of work to do in his room; rolling his eyes and making a *moue,* to indicate that he meant mathematics, or possibly Latin. Her sudden sense of having been left in a desert of personal inactivity was dispelled by the arrival of the mail, which was brought by a youth on a bicycle. There was a letter for her from Veronica (she had got herself a new job, as secretary to a junior minister) and a thick envelope from

Nathan Yardley's publishers, which contained fan mail. She threw herself into the job of replying to them all, and was sticking down the last envelope flap when the telephone gave a cracked tinkle.

"It's Dr. Negretti."

"Oh!"

"Good news, *signorina*. The X-rays reveal no concussion, and there is no permanent damage to the knee. Just rather a lot of fluid. Nothing that a few days' rest won't cure. Unhappily, Sr. Yardley didn't have a good night, but he's sleeping right now. They won't disturb him, but, if he wakes in time, the ambulance will bring him home this evening. All right?"

She thanked him. So Nathan was probably coming home this evening (she was already thinking of him as Nathan: "Let it creep in when you feel right about it," he'd said), in—what?— six hours? seven hours?

She remembered the *principessa's* invitation to tea, and decided to go. It would be—she searched for a phrase—a way to bridge the emptiness till Nathan's return.

The absurd phrase had sprung, ready-made, into her mind; she repeated it, aloud, to herself in the mirror. And wondered why.

Natasha went down to the village. There was a certain amount of traffic on the road: She was passed by a honking bus labelled for Salerno, two nuns on bicycles, and a woman in dusty black driving along a tired donkey laden with panniers of lemons.

She kept to the coast road, firmly setting her face once more against the street of steps that went through the warren of tenements (so like the prison drawings of Piranese, and why hadn't she noticed it before?). Down in the square, pink-faced

German tourists crowded the tables outside the café, and ate fruit-speckled ice cream.

Out of the sun's heat and in the shadow of cool stonework, everything seemed very still as she walked in the direction of the basilican church, which stood at the top of a wide flight of steps. An old priest in soutane and biretta came out from the ancient, blackened stone porch and down the steps, nodding benignly to the tourists who sat there, grouped in patches of colour.

The palazzo commanded the rising ground behind the basilica. One reached it by plodding up an insanely steep curve of narrow street that swept, like some nightmare carriage drive, up past the porticoed door and down again to the apse end of the basilica, without the assistance of a single step. Natasha wondered how the aged *principessa* ever made it; she herself was breathless and glowing by the time she reached the top. There, she brought down a lion-headed knocker upon a great bronze door, and examined the sculptured figures that gesticulated in niches flanking the door: One was a half-nude nymph; the other was male, ecclesiastical, and censorious-looking.

"Good afternoon, madame. Graciously enter, please."

The door had opened very quietly, so that she was caught unawares. The man on the threshold was in his early twenties, blond-haired, muscular, and pallid as a corpse; with faded blue eyes so far inclined towards pale violet as to have pink lights. He was wearing a see-through string singlet and recklessly brief shorts. She docketed him as Scandinavian, and possibly an albino.

"This way, madame, please."

The young albino led her through a gloomy hallway and past an arch that looked out onto an inner courtyard blanched with sunlight and littered with pieces of broken masonry and sculpture. There was more debris stacked along the walls of the echoing corridor along which she next followed her guide: heads and torsos, and dismembered marble arms frozen in gesticulation. The sole item of soft furnishing that Natasha could see was a marquetry sofa, with horsehair stuffing bursting out of its rotting silk covering. And, over all, there hung the musty smell of damp and decay.

He knocked on a tall door and, opening it, stood aside to let her in.

"The English madame, *principessa*," he murmured.

"Thank you, Willem. Come in, and let's have a little chinwag, my dear." The Principessa Adelina Josefa was a grey ghost in a grey room. She had discarded the all-black ensemble for a long white dress and gloves, though age had long since brought their whiteness to subtle greys and dusty yellows, and these tones were repeated in the discoloured limewashed walls of the room, which was lit by the shafts of muted sunlight coming through the slats in the shuttered windows.

As the old woman moved across to greet Natasha, gloved hands outstretched, the ruched lace at her skirt hem caught against, and upset, a spindly table, which, in its turn, brought down a faience vase. None of this was allowed to check the *principessa's* stately progress by so much as a glance; as she took Natasha's hand in hers, the albino ducked past her, bowing low, on his way to pick up the broken shards from the tiled floor.

"You look peaky, and a little tired about the eyes, my dear. I must tell Dr. Negretti to call and see you."

"I didn't sleep very well last night," explained Natasha. "I was rather upset about losing that little white kitten I had with me when we met." And she told her new friend the bare details of the small tragedy.

The *principessa* threw up her hands in a gesture of understanding and sympathy. "You address one who has suffered the loss of many loved ones, my dear," she said. "I do not speak, of course, of the passing of my husband, Prince Ercole; for our relationship scarcely had time to progress beyond the limits of a certain mutual esteem. Come, I will show you." And, taking Natasha's arm, she led her to a framed portrait in oils that hung on the wall opposite the windows. "This was Prince Ercole."

A frail and childish face looked out at them, nervous eyes shaded by the heavy peak of a braided military cap.

"He died in the first war," said the *principessa*. "On the Piave front. Not from bullets, I would mention, but of consumption. He was only nineteen, and we had been married two months."

The albino was hovering, cradling the fragments of the vase in his arms, like a baby.

"When will the *principessa* require teas serving, please?" Addressing his mistress, he laid his head on one side and gave a grin that revealed two front teeth inlaid with a heart and a diamond of gold.

"In half an hour, Willem," said the *principessa*. She turned to Natasha. "The artist who is painting my likeness—Mr. Ballard—is joining us for tea at five-thirty, my dear. I think you will like him . . ." she took Natasha's arm, ". . . I allowed half an hour to show you round the palazzo, and for a little chinwag. Come, my dear."

Natasha met the albino's pink-tinted eyes over the *principessa's* shoulder. He flashed his gold inlays and gave her a broad wink.

"Willem is a treasure," said the *principessa*, "and quite indispensable to my establishment. Indeed, he is the only servant I have at this time. Willem has beautiful manners. I attribute this to his former calling, which was that of seaman. He is a Dutchman from Amsterdam, and he voyaged extensively, particularly in the East. This is the chapel. It is consecrated, of course. In his capacity as my chaplain, Fra Pietro comes and says Mass weekly. Isn't it truly charming, don't you think?"

The tiny chapel of the palazzo was High Baroque inclining to Churrigueresque, dominated by a reredos of crumbling plasterwork that rose—gilded and painted and roof-high—behind the altar. Only a little sunlight struggled in through the grimed glass of a single window, but Natasha was able to make out a three-dimensional composition of saints and angels, soaring up towards a Holy Infant in a painted sky.

Four steps took them from the door to the altar rail, where a closer view of the saints and angels showed them to have carved and painted tears on their dirty cheeks. Natasha peered round the diminutive chamber for something upon which to make a bright and appreciative comment, and saw a promising-looking shape under the window—a monument, or possibly a tomb.

*Principe Ercole di Roberti*
*Tenente della Guardia Reale*
*1898–1917*

The inscribed marble base supported a recumbent effigy under a glass case. Natasha accepted this also as marble, till she got closer and saw that the figure had to be of wax, because it was dressed in a heavily frogged, dun-coloured uniform.

The *principessa* touched a switch, and a bare electric bulb lit up inside the case. Natasha winced with distaste. The effigy was pathetically unlifelike: a miniature figure, scarcely bigger than a ten-year-old child, lying on a discoloured lace mattress, surrounded by dusty paper flowers. It represented— of course—her hostess's late husband. The thing had been incredibly badly done: a travesty. Even allowing for her short-sightedness, how could the poor old duck bear to have such a thing lying around?

"He was so little," murmured the *principessa*. "The smallest officer in the Guards. His Majesty called him '*mio soldatino*.' My poor Ercole."

The effigy had been modelled—how long?—over fifty years ago. It must have been ill-shaped and out of scale to the human body when it was made; the passing of time alone couldn't account for the awfulness of it, though it probably explained the nose, which was lacking some interior propping and was grotesquely askew.

"It was not a love match between us, you understand, my dear. Such a thing would be unthinkable, even today, in both our families. You would scarcely believe it, but he danced beautifully. And he also whistled—a truly accomplished *siffleur*."

The boots had never been walked in; the leather of soles and uppers alike were crazed all over with fine cracks, like the surface of an old oil painting.

"The order that you see round his shoulders is that of St. Maurice and St. Lazarus, which always looked too big and heavy for him, and the more so now."

There was a sparse, pale moustache on the waxen upper lip; peering closer, Natasha could see every delicate bristle, in jewel-like detail, connected to the surface. She suddenly felt her scalp crawl.

"We had better resume our little tour, or Mr. Ballard will be here before we have finished." The *principessa's* voice was slightly muffled. Natasha—searching for phrases to shape an awful question that had just come to her—glanced at the old woman, expecting to see tears, but the *principessa* was unconcernedly sucking a sugared almond; the violet-tinted confection slid playfully in and out between her fine teeth, guided by a very pink tongue. Natasha left the minute chapel with her companion's arm tucked in hers—and her awful question unasked.

"Your Mr. Yardley has known bereavement. The wife was taken from him some years ago, as you may know. I had an acquaintance with her when she first came to the Villa Gaspari, before she was married to Mr. Yardley, and afterwards."

"What was she like?" asked Natasha, intrigued.

The *principessa* either didn't hear the question, or chose to ignore it. "I am rather belatedly reading Mr. Yardley's famous book," she said, irrelevantly. "I began it only yesterday, for, though I have some competence in the spoken word, I read English much less well. So I decided to wait till the publication of the Italian edition. This staircase leads to my bedroom and dressing rooms. Please precede me, my dear."

The bedroom was lined with ivory-coloured brocade that was blotched with green dampness on the outer walls and faded to off-white on the inner. Long windows looked out, past the massive columns of the palazzo's façade, across the village and the bay, as far as the pantiled roofs of the Villa Gaspari. The old woman closed the shutters, blanking out the sun and the blueness in a swirl of dust.

"The bed was given to an ancestor of the prince by one of the Medici," she said, "but I forget which Medici. It is quite comfortable."

It was a double bed with a baldachin of carved and inlaid woods, hung and draped with threadbare brocades, and surmounted by a coat of arms on a plaster cartouche that was borne by a pair of cherubs. Natasha touched the hangings, and immediately sensed the dust—invisible in the shuttered room —lightly prickling the membranes at the back of her nose.

The *principessa* had crossed to the other side of the bed

from Natasha. A match flared, and the *principessa* lit a candle that stood, together with a pile of books, on the side table there. She picked up the book from the top of the pile, and Natasha saw the author's name blazoned across the dust jacket: *YARDLEY*.

"In the Italian edition, they have entitled it: *Guardarsi dall' Orgoglio*," said the *principessa*. "I have read a little of the first chapter, and I think Mr. Yardley is to be congratulated. I learn that he has had an accident. Is there further news, my dear?"

"There are no complications, and he's coming home this evening," said Natasha, absently. She had been staring down at the books on the table at her side of the bed.

"I am glad to hear that," said the *principessa*. "Authorship is a fragile and fugitive accomplishment, easily disturbed by adverse circumstances. What little I have read of Mr. Yardley . . ."

There were two books for the person who slept on this side of the bed, Natasha observed. One was a much-thumbed and dog-eared copy of a girlie magazine, the other an American science fiction comic. There was also a crumpled packet of cigarettes and an ashtray filled with twisted stubs. Somewhere out of vision, the old woman's vibrant contralto was still rolling out literary platitudes. It was unbelievable. Then the *principessa* was asking her something.

"I expect you agree, my dear?"

"Yes," replied Natasha, and, her companion's watchful expression seeming to be calling for further amplification, "to a certain degree, this is my own opinion," she added, hopefully.

"Well, that is very interesting," said the *principessa*. "And I shall certainly bear that in mind, when next I meet Mr. Yardley."

The tenuous discussion was cut short by a fingernail tap on

the double doors, and Willem came in. In the gloom of the shuttered room, only his nipples, through the string vest, stood out darkly against the general pallor of his big body.

"The English gentleman has come, and is in the salon, *principessa.*"

"Thank you, Willem." She took Natasha's arm again. "Shall we join Mr. Ballard, my dear. I think you will find him quite entertaining, as most creative people are. But I am glad we had time for our private little chin-wag."

The albino stood aside to let them pass, and Natasha deliberately avoided his gaze.

The salon was the room into which she had first been shown by Willem; and her first impression of Robert Ballard was of a tall figure in a faded blue denim suit, who slowly turned and appraised her from top to bottom.

The *principessa* introduced them, and the artist's big hand took Natasha's in a cool and surprisingly gentle grip. He looked to be in his mid-thirties. His hair was the colour of good orange marmalade, his skin russet-brown—and he had disconcerting grey eyes. She had to drop her gaze, and despised herself for it.

"She's better looking than the other one," said Ballard. "I'll have a drawing of her."

The remark—delivered in a flat Midlands accent with a bass growl—brought a crinkling at the corner of the *principessa's* eye nearest to Natasha that was half-way to a wink of complicity. "That will be topping," she said. "Why not now? Let us hold back tea for half an hour, and chat while Mr. Ballard is working. Lead the way, Mr. Ballard."

They followed him through a curtained archway, at the far end of the room, that led into a tiled patio of sunshine and shade. There was a stretched canvas on a tall easel and a low table littered with painting gear.

"You should be flattered, my dear," the *principessa* murmured in Natasha's ear. "There are many ladies in the district, notable for either their beauty or distinction, or both, whom he has *not* offered to draw."

The partly finished picture on the canvas was life-size—a waist-length portrait of the Principessa Adelina Josefa sitting in a straight-backed chair, hands folded on lap, and gazing out quizzically at the beholder. It was a good likeness of the old aristocrat, and, as far as Natasha's judgement took her, was stylishly and sensitively painted. She remembered reading somewhere that Robert Ballard was a member of the Art Establishment, with a reputation for outspoken support of the avant-garde.

Ballard nodded towards the model's chair, and picked up a sketchbook from the painting table. "Make yourself comfortable," he said. "Talk and waggle your head about as much as you like, but don't move your hands. I can't cope with hands unless they're still as marble."

"The complete artist!" cried the *principessa*. "So full of paradoxes!" She giggled girlishly.

He drew standing up, the lower edge of the book resting against his out-thrust left hip.

Silence.

Natasha counted up to ten, and then said: "Do you live out here, Mr. Ballard? Or are you a summer visitor?"

It was the old woman who replied: "Mr. Ballard has a studio villa on the road to Amalfi. We have the pleasure of his company for most of the year."

Silence.

"One hears that you had the police at the Villa Gaspari yesterday," said the *principessa*. "A reputable gossip told Willem that vandals had removed the girl's corpse."

"Stop fidgeting your fingers," growled Ballard.

"Sorry," said Natasha. A sidelong glance revealed that the old woman was regarding her through her lorgnette. "No, the coffin wasn't disturbed. I suppose the whole story's been blown up out of all proportion and spread all over the countryside."

"Oh, yes," said the *principessa*. "I shouldn't wonder if certain versions of it aren't being discussed as far away as Naples. The people have a marvellous facility for disseminating news by word of mouth."

"In this case it would have to be strictly by word of mouth," said Ballard. He shaded a piece of the drawing with his spatulate thumb, and cocked his head on one side to eye it narrowly. "The case hasn't reached the Naples press—or, at least, they haven't reported it. Possibly Pinturicchio's clamped down on the story. I wonder why."

"Surely he couldn't do that," said Natasha. And now they were both staring at her, and the artist's hand was still. Suddenly it seemed to her that the tea party had turned into an interrogation—and there was still no tea. "Well, I mean," she continued lamely, "the police could hardly have imposed censorship on a public hearing like an inquest, could they?"

"Inquest?" The *principessa* examined the concept like a new acquaintance—and decided to give it the cut direct.

"There was no inquest," said Ballard. "This isn't England. You won't find anything like our Coroners' Courts anywhere on the Continent. I made a point of checking on this. Sudden and unnatural death is investigated only when there's manifest suspicion of crime, and an autopsy can only be authorised by an investigating judge. None of this applied in Susannah Hislop's case. She simply fell out of a high window, and was buried with dispatch on account of the heat. . . ." The unwavering grey eyes held her glance. "Do *you* read anything further than that into the situation?"

Natasha firmly shut out the recollection of the boy Guido's threatening taunt. "No, I don't," she said. "Did you know Susannah Hislop well?"

No reply.

Presently, the *principessa* said: "The dear child suffered an upsetting bereavement last night. Her little kitten. A sweet thing. She had it with her when we first met."

"Oh, yes?" said Ballard.

"It fell from a window."

"Did it now?"

At that moment, Willem padded in through the curtained archway with a heavily laden tray, for which Ballard cleared a space on the table. The *principessa* poured tea from a silver pot, and Ballard tossed his sketchbook onto the floor by Natasha's feet. She looked down at the drawing, which was quite unflattering: It over-emphasised the strong structure of her cheekbones and jawline, and made her look masculine. The hands, too, folded in repose, were strongly moulded and—awful term—capable-looking. Natasha decided that Ballard did not like her. She had, by now, thoroughly decided that she didn't like him. Too farouche for words, she thought. And he and the *principessa* are definitely up to something—I was invited here for no other reason than to be pumped about the business up in the graveyard. Well, I will *not* provide fodder for local gossip. They'll get nothing out of me.

"Did you see it fall?" asked Ballard. "The kitten, I mean."

She shook her head. "I'd rather not talk about it, if you don't mind."

It was six-ten by her watch. She drained her cup of lemon tea, while composing suitable phrases of thanks and farewell. Perhaps she wouldn't be invited again, and that was just fine by her. Maybe, now, she would never know for sure if the young Dutch albino slept with his aged mistress, or if the *principessa* really did keep the mummified body of her long-dead boy-husband on show in the family chapel under a glass case: She would simply have to go through life in tantalizing ignorance.

The drawing presented no impediment to her departure; though details of her dress and the chair-back were summarily blocked in, the face and hands had a steely precision. Ballard could hardly seize upon that as an excuse to keep her any longer.

"Well, I really must be going," she began. "We're expecting Mr. Yardley back from the . . ."

"Do you remember that other distressing incident at the Villa Gaspari, Mr. Ballard?" The *principessa's* vibrant contralto soared above Natasha's remark in a triumphant diapason.

"Mmmm. Yes." A lock of the artist's marmalade-coloured hair had flopped over his forehead, obscuring his lowered eyes. "But I don't remember the details. Was it a dog or a cat?"

"Oh, it was a dog. One saw Miss Hislop exercising the little thing in the village. Off-white, as I recall, or some such light colour. Very sprightly. She would not, of course, have been allowed to take it back to England, because of quarantine restrictions. However, unhappily, the contingency was never to arise." The berry-black old falcon's eyes slewed round to regard Natasha.

"Quite," growled Ballard.

It was like a cheap ventriloquism act, thought Natasha, with a badly rehearsed cross-talk script that had been cobbled together in a hurry to simulate an impromptu. Yet, who was the performer, and who the dummy? With a growing apprehension of what was going to come, she measured the distance to the door, weighed the problem of disposing of the delicate cup and saucer she was still holding, and toyed with—and finally rejected—the probability of her being able to out-call the *principessa* with the remainder of her farewell speech. It was all no use; there was no escape.

"So sad, my dear," said the old woman remorselessly. "And, considering all things, a quite remarkable coincidence, don't you think?"

"I really don't know what you mean, *principessa*," lied Natasha.

"Well! That is remarkable!" The *principessa* appealed to Ballard. "Do you not think it is remarkable, Mr. Ballard, that none of the people at the Villa Gaspari should have mentioned to this dear child—even *en passant*—that her predecessor's pet animal also . . . ?"

"Please, *principessa*," pleaded Natasha. "I think I know what you're going to tell me. I'm sure you mean it for the best, but it's hardly of any interest now . . ." She took a deep breath and got to her feet, laying the cup and saucer carefully back on to the tray ". . . except to malicious local gossips from here to Naples!" she added meaningfully. "And now, I really must go."

The old aristocrat was not put out of countenance by so much as a twitch of a facial muscle. Stretching up the white wattles of her neck, she merely adjusted her gaze, to take in the standing figure of the angry girl. "A week before her own tragedy," she said. "A week before she died, Miss Hislop's dog —it was a small dog of some light colour, and the name of the breed evades me at the moment—was found drowned on the beach below the villa. . . ."

"*Principessa*, I . . ."

"The girl was considerably upset, and took the creature's death as a portent of her own. Mr. Ballard, here . . ."

"*Principessa!*" flared Natasha. The old woman's eyes widened with affront, and Natasha continued, quietly: "Please. The facts of Susannah Hislop's death, of her dog's drowning, and my kitten falling off a window sill: I think I know what you're trying to tell me, both of you, but there's not a shred of evidence to connect them. Nothing except the pure coincidence that she and the kitten fell from the same window. And what happened to the dog is completely unrelated; dogs—and people too—get themselves drowned every day."

"I'd go along with that, but for one thing," said Ballard. And, suddenly, Natasha knew who of the two of them was the performer and who the dummy. "The dog wasn't accidently drowned—*it was found in the shallows with its legs tied together with electrical flex.*"

"You rang, *principessa?*"

The albino was hovering in the archway.

"Yes. Would you show Miss—er—Collingwood out, please, Willem?" She gave Natasha both of her small, plump hands. "You must come and see me again soon. And, please, mention to Mr. Yardley that I hope to be calling on him one day to discuss matters literary." And then—irrelevant to the last: "I much admire your shoes. Very fine. In general, Englishwomen are very uncaring about their shoes."

## 7

"Of course! That's how it must have happened. How else?"

She ran her hand along the window sill, which, despite the additional courses of stonework, was of a height well within the compass of an agile kitten's leap; yet narrow and smooth enough, on top, to provide a treacherous perch for a little creature lying there, drugged to sleep by the afternoon sun. An unguarded movement could carry it to destruction before the arresting claws could spring out of the velvety pads. She shuddered and looked down. Yes, it had to have happened like that; any other theory was quite insupportable. The *principessa* and Ballard were nothing but a pair of idle, gossiping muckrakers.

As for the poor dog of Susannah Hislop's—one didn't have to look farther than the vile urchins of the village tenements for possible perpetrators of that act of mindless sadism.

But, to forge any connection between the drowning of the dog and the kitten's death, let alone Susannah's . . .

And I'm not simply sweeping it under the carpet and hoping it will go away, she told her reflection in the mirror. It's a matter of logic. Murder is still a pretty rare occurrence; the probability of getting mixed up in a murder (and let's face it—if you're connecting the three deaths, as Ballard and the old woman are, you're talking about murder) is very, very thin compared to accidental death, which could happen next time one crosses a road, mends a fuse, or—comes out of a shower with wet feet and slips on a tile.

And yet . . . for some reason or other, according to the *principessa,* Susannah's reaction to the killing of the dog had been most strange. What was the phrase?—a portent of her own death?

It was then—shortly after seven-thirty—that there was a rattle at the entrance gates, and Natasha heard Giulietta running barefoot up the steps from the kitchen quarters to answer it.

They had brought Nathan home.

Her hair was as lank and greasy as a fishwife's, and she should have washed and dried it when she arrived home from the *principessa's,* instead of wasting time with all those senseless speculations. She attacked it with a brush, then recklessly backcombed it, to give it some body. It remained obstinately bodiless, so she tied it up in a large spotted handkerchief. And the *principessa* had been right: She looked tired and peaky—and in an insipid, not a romantically interesting, kind of way.

Nathan Yardley and his stretcher, borne by two sweating ambulance men, had reached the bottom of the steps before she joined him. There was a stark-white strip of sticking plaster on his right cheekbone, and his face looked very brave and gay and bronzed. She was uncomfortably aware of a quickening of her pulse and breathing that could only partly be accounted for, surely, by running down the steps.

He grinned. "How's everything? They won't be taking off my kneecap after all."

"I heard," she said. "And I'm so glad."

The men eased the stretcher in through the door of his room. Eric appeared and took hold of the side of the stretcher, to prevent it from jolting against the door frame. He looked flushed and happy: He met Natasha's glance and beamed at her.

"We've missed him, haven't we, Natasha? We've missed you, Nathan."

"I should have more accidents," said Yardley. He winced when the men picked him up and transferred him to the bed.

Eric looked solicitous. "Is it awfully painful, Nathan?"

"Quite a bit, but I'm perfectly able to walk on it," said Yardley. "The only reason for all this rigmarole is to rest the blessed thing, so that the swelling goes down and the fluid disperses, or whatever it does. Natasha, I'm hungry."

"I'll fix something for you," said Natasha. "What do you fancy?"

The ambulance men folded up their stretcher, nodded, grinned, and saluted her. She supposed that they were expecting a tip, but she had left her handbag in her room. Suddenly, she was confused. They went out, muttering together.

"I'm not fussy," said Yardley. "If you'd just ask Maria to hurry dinner along, I'm content to wait for that."

"I'll go along to the kitchen now," she said.

"And Natasha . . ."

"Yes?" She paused at the door.

"Make it for two, and have your dinner with me, in here. Okay?"

Her back was towards him, and her left hand was resting against the door jamb, just in front of her eyes. Surprised at her own detachment, she saw a thin line of pale skin appear from under her watch strap, in contrast with the new tan that she had already picked up in Italy.

"All right, Nathan," she said.

But it wasn't all right; the way she found herself reacting was just plain damn stupid.

Dinner was delicate young mussels that the Capucci womenfolk had gathered that afternoon from the water pools in the rocks beneath the villa, followed by a stridently flavoured omelette with a watercress salad. They drank a white Chianti;

and, during the coffee and cognac, Natasha Collingwood, bachelor of arts and spinster of the parish of St. Marylebone, decided (after making due allowance for the wine and the brandy) that she was possibly more than half in love with the author of *Pride Goes Before*.

They were in candlelight; he was propped up against his pillows; she had relieved him of his dinner tray, and had left the chair and table at his bedside for a little button-back armchair by the open window, with a view of the firefly-speckled sea. Yardley was talking about himself. Natasha reflected, with some amusement, that her primary instincts were not blinding her to the undoubted fact that he enjoyed talking about himself just as much as she enjoyed listening to him.

The burden of his monologue was success.

"Popular success," he said, "is almost impossible to budget for. It's as insubstantial as gossamer and about as hard-wearing; yet, put it on, and you feel protected against all the cold winds that the whole world could blow at you. Never to have been successful is to have only half lived; once you've experienced success, it's quite indispensable.

"I, Natasha, am a man who nearly didn't make it. At thirty-eight, I was an actor, quite a good actor: the sort who eats three square meals a day and keeps on good terms with his tailor; with the sort of face of which you say, when you pass it in the street, 'Wasn't he the chap who played with whatsis-name in that TV play the other week?'"

"I remember you before 'Tell Me Another,'" interposed Natasha. "It was in my first year at college. You read a serial story in one of the women's programmes on the TV. It was *Wuthering Heights* and you read it beautifully. You caused quite a stir; you were the rave of our students' common room."

"I love you all," said Yardley. "Actually, I didn't work for nearly a year after that. That little glowworm of fame nearly extinguished me completely. There was no follow-up of attractive offers, you see, and I had priced myself out of the sort of supporting parts that had always been my bread and butter. Ten months after my last appearance on that woman's programme, I was eating one meal a day in a cheap cafeteria and crossing the street to avoid meeting my tailor. By this time, a whole lot of new boys were ahead of me in the queue for the bread-and-butter jobs; my agent was always on the other extension, always going to take me out to lunch, but not today, old man.

"Ahead of me stretched an existence that was compounded of nude modelling in art schools, Santa Claus in Christmas fairs at department stores; bed-sitting rooms in run-down houses in run-down streets, sharing dingy bathrooms with ex-principal boys and French letter salesmen; a downhill run to a pauper's grave, with the stink of fish-and-chips and boiled cabbage all the way."

"Then came 'Tell Me Another,'" said Natasha.

"Then, indeed, came 'Tell Me Another,'" he said. "And my nascent fame had an unlikely parentage. Birmingham was my home town, and I was sent as a day-boy to a local minor public school. Not the show-biz network, but the old school tie got me into that programme. Derek van Cuyp, the producer of what was then a quiz show that had never really got off the ground, had been my captain of cricket at school, and we bumped into each other on the very day that the show's anchor man collapsed and was rushed into London Clinic. Derek took a chance with me, and it paid off for us both.

"At the end of that first show, I tasted instant fame. People —quite important people, for whom I'd never existed—were lighting my cigarette and marvelling how it was that we'd never met.

"By the time that first show had finished, Natasha, it didn't matter that the poor devil for whom I was standing in was found to be dying of inoperable cancer—he would never have got his job back, anyhow. Does that sound heartless? I went to his funeral; bad conscience took me there."

The candle flames wavered, and Natasha closed the shutters against the night breeze. He poured them both some brandy, and continued:

"To be able to slam the door on a vision of certain dissolution is very heady stuff for a man of pushing forty, Natasha. In place of posing in the nude at the art school, there were suddenly yachts and limousines; complaisant starlets and obsequious waiters; bills that simply didn't *need* to be paid.

"I went round the world. Saw the Southern Cross, and the Sugar Loaf towering out of the sea of mist in Rio bay; blew enough to feed a family of six for a year in one night of Monte Carlo; as for the Golden Gates of Samarkand . . ." they both laughed at his allusion to the scandalous and much-quoted opening of *Pride Goes Before* ". . . I was there, too, Natasha. It took me just a year to break out of the honeymoon period of my instant success. After that, I was bright enough to take stock of myself and look around for some roots. My solution was marriage. I married an intelligent and extremely beautiful divorcée, who presented me with a ready-made family. On balance, I think that if I were given the chance, I would do it all over again. Poor Anna."

Another reference to the dead wife—the second that Natasha had heard that day. But why poor Anna? She waited for him to continue.

"There are some people in this world," he said, "who, on the face of it, seem to have everything going for them—birth, money, position, beauty. Yet, in fact, they have practically nothing. My wife Anna was one of these.

"She was an American. A poor little rich girl, dragged up

by a succession of nursemaids and step-mothers. At eighteen, she ducked out of her appalling background by marrying an English playboy named Aubrey Neville (by the way, Eric and Amanda have taken the name Neville-Yardley), who ran away with a showgirl while she was pregnant with Eric. She was married to me for three years, which couldn't have brought her a lot of happiness, and she was only thirty-one when she died. Can you think of a more rotten way of spending a life?"

Intuitively, Natasha knew that there was more that he wanted to tell her. His question hung in the air, but it was scarcely one that she could answer with any propriety. She resolved her dilemma by reaching for a platitude:

"Eric and Amanda must miss her very much. You must miss her very much."

He emptied his brandy glass. When he answered her, his grey-flecked head remained bowed, looking down into the glass. And his voice was strained.

"My wife died of cirrhosis of the liver. She had been an alcoholic ever since the breakdown of her first marriage. Yes, I miss her. She was a very wonderful person. It tore me apart to see her destroying herself, and being unable to do anything to help—apart from nosing out the hidden Scotch bottles and keeping as much of the unpleasantness as possible away from the children. She was a secret alcoholic, you see. And, in a manner of speaking, a remarkably successful one: She always looked marvellous, and carried herself well; no slurred speech and falling about. Only I and a handful of intimates—and her doctor, of course—knew about her problem. My publicity people made sure that the press didn't get wind of it.

"To this day, I'm pretty sure that Eric and Amanda don't know the background to Mummy's sudden retreats to bed. And they think—the whole world thinks—that she died of cancer. Anna would have wanted it that way; she was deeply ashamed of her illness."

He loved her, thought Natasha. And he must have loved her very much to have protected her so devotedly, even beyond the grave.

"This is in confidence, of course, Natasha," said Yardley. "As between artists."

He smiled at her, and Natasha felt tall enough to reach up and touch the stars.

As between artists. She blessed him aloud for reviving her poor, faded ambition. Us writers have got to stick together.

It was nearly midnight, and Natasha was in bed, but still awake and restless—euphoric, even—and conscious of having drunk too much brandy, which always over-stimulated her.

As between artists. She closed her eyes, and the bed tilted gently backwards on an axis somewhere near her waist; the wave of vertigo made her sit up and focus on the pattern of stars that were framed in her open window.

She had said good night to Nathan quite early. He had seemed suddenly to tire after confiding in her about his dead wife, and was almost asleep when she had tiptoed out. Her memory of him was of a lean, recumbent figure in a grey silk dressing gown, hands folded on his breast, face in profile: The association with an effigy of a Crusader knight was irresistible. "I really am," she said aloud, "I really am being too schoolgirlish for words about that man!"

The scream rose from out of the canyon of the sea below. It came up to her, long and drawn-out, and quavering at its end. A moment of silence (time for her to swing her legs from the bed and bound across the room towards the window), and the same awful cry was repeated in a higher key.

Lights snapped on all over the Villa Gaspari. The yard of

the kitchen quarters below was suddenly illuminated from a bedroom window, and she heard old Mario call out in querulous alarm. A door slammed. Clear on the night air came Eric's voice, demanding to know what was the matter.

Natasha snatched up her dressing gown and rushed outside; she was still tying the waistband when she reached the lowest level of the villa. Eric was already there, by the oleander, peering, white-faced in the moonlight, down to the beach. She reached out to him and touched his shoulder. He was trembling.

"Someone's down there!" His teeth were chattering. "Down there by the wall. Look!"

He was right. Standing upright against the rough stone wall at the top of the beach—in the same spot where she had seen Amanda on the first morning—was a slight, shrouded figure that could only be a woman. Her face and skirt stood out whitely against the dark stonework.

"It's Giulietta!" said Eric.

They went down the steps to the beach, and approached the girl; Eric walking quickly, with Natasha having to run, bare feet sinking in the cool sand, to keep at his elbow.

"Giulietta! What's the matter?" cried Eric. "Oh, God! Look at her!"

The girl wore a light-coloured skirt and a black blouse. Hands thrust behind her back, she stood with her head lolled against the wall, slack-mouthed and staring-eyed.

"Giulietta!" cried Eric.

The eyes wavered in their direction, and she seemed to be aware of them for the first time. And she screamed into their faces. Again, and again.

"Stop it! Pull yourself together!" Natasha seized the girl by the shoulders and shook her; Giulietta's bones were finely formed under her soft flesh. There was no checking her screams. Others were coming down onto the beach to join them: dark forms flickering across the light-coloured sand and the black rocks.

"What the hell's going on?" That was Amanda.

"It's Giulietta. She's had some sort of fright," replied Eric. "Come over here and see if you can get any sense out of her."

The girl's screams diminished to a shrill keening. She firmly resisted Natasha's attempts to soothe her, arching her back and drawing away when Natasha's arm slipped round her shoulders. And she kept her hands hidden.

Amanda roughly elbowed Natasha aside. The keening was shut off in a shocked intake of breath, as the flat palm of a hand landed across the girl's cheek in an explosion of sound.

"Be quiet, you little fool!"

Giulietta was crying now, head bowed and hair falling across her breast, hands still behind her back.

"What is it? What happened to you?"

"Gu-Guido . . ."

"Guido? What? Don't tell me he's raped you. You told me only the other day that you were pregnant by him. What about Guido?"

The girl pointed—down towards the water's edge and the oily rollers sliding in past the dark rocks. Others were already down there: There was a hoarse shout of alarm from old Mario, followed by a woman's scream.

Then Natasha was running with Amanda and Eric down towards the shoreline, where the old man and Giulietta's mother were huddled together by a humped shape that bobbed in the eddies. When they reached it, a wave withdrew, hissing through the shingle, leaving behind the prone figure of a man in a dark shirt and trousers. Not a man—a youth. Natasha recognised the profile, with shocked surprise, as that of Guido. He looked smaller than she remembered him, and quite different. She had had no first-hand experience of the freshly dead (poor Mimi Middleton had killed herself with sleeping pills while on a lone holiday in the Camargue), but the thing at her feet was so different from the living creature she had known as Guido as to be undoubtedly dead.

"Nothing can be done for him!" wailed Mario. "He is drowned."

"We'd better drag the body up the beach," said Amanda. "Come on, you two. Don't leave *everything* to me!"

Tentatively, Natasha reached down and took hold of an ankle. Eric seized an arm. At that moment, a spent wave sluiced past them, soaking them to the knees and lifting the body in its grasp.

"Keep hold of it!" shouted Amanda. "Don't let it be carried out to sea."

When the wave retreated again, the three of them were holding their burden clear above the shingle. As they walked with it, the body trailed fronds of what might have been seaweed. Only it wasn't seaweed.

"Oh, my God!" wailed Amanda.

As one, they dropped the body, and Eric doubled up and was violently sick in the shallows.

"What is it? What have you got down there?"

Nathan Yardley stood at the bottom of the steps, leaning for support against a balustrade. He still wore the grey dressing gown, and his hair was wild in the night breeze.

Natasha ran towards him.

"What is it, Natasha?"

"Guido," she said. "He's dead. I—I don't know what happened, but he's dead. I'd better ring the police, hadn't I, Nathan?"

Yardley passed a hand across his brow. "Yes, I suppose you'd better do that, my dear," he said, wearily.

Down by the stone wall, the girl had resumed her low wailing.

## 8

It rained before morning: a teeming downpour that brought
the accumulated, dry red sand from the eaves and gutters of
the Villa Gaspari and carried it down the steps in liquid mud.
The hills that formed the peninsula's backbone were hidden
from the coast by the tumbled storm clouds. It made no difference to the comings and goings of the local people; before
first light, the old women in black walked down from the hills,
through the drenching rain, with their great baskets of lemons.
Lights burned in the village *polizia* all night.

After having made Nathan comfortable, Natasha had not
slept; the police activity had precluded that. At about nine
o'clock, she answered the phone, and it was a police officer
who introduced himself as Sergeant Rizzio: would the *signorina* be so kind as to present herself to the village *polizia* at
her earliest convenience, to assist Inspector Pinturicchio? Yes,
she would.

The police station was a single-storey, stucco-fronted block
backing onto the square. A very clean tricolour flag hung wetly
over the door, and a young constable wearing a pistol belt was
delicately sweeping the porch with a besom; at the sight of
Natasha, he laid it against the wall and saluted her.

The place consisted of a general office, a small lock-up, and
an inner office, into which her guide conducted Natasha. Pinturicchio was seated at a small desk that his bulk grossly over-
powered, a telephone receiver tucked under his fleshy jaw,
violin-fashion. He looked up and gave her a nod—then went

back to scribbling notes on a pad and carrying out a staccato conversation with the person on the other end:

"Time of death was when? No earlier than nine. Okay, doc. Cause? Knife slash. Yes, we have the knife, it was found in the shallows. A kitchen knife. Evisceration? Okay. Any special skill required for this? A baby could do it? You must know some weird babies, doc! Nothing else? You'll let me have a more accurate time of death later? All right. Thanks. *Ciao*, doc . . ." he replaced the receiver, glanced up at Natasha, smacked his forehead with the palm of his hand, and smoothly switched languages. "Sorry you heard all that, Miss Collingwood. I forgot you speak Italian so well. Please sit down. I think they keep a spare chair in this rabbit hutch somewhere. . . . Rizzio!"

Sergeant Rizzio was the uniformed officer who had accompanied Pinturicchio on his first visit to the Villa Gaspari, after the violation of Susannah Hislop's grave: It seemed an age ago now. He produced a chair, and she sat down.

Pinturicchio's dark gaze swarmed down her figure and back again. He was still affecting the pinched waist and unbuttoned look, smelt strongly of an aromatic shaving lotion, and each individual wiry hair of his scalp gleamed blackly with brilliantine. If a predator, then well-barbered, she thought.

"Well, how is everyone taking it up at the villa?" he asked.

"Sra. Capucci was in a state of collapse all night, but recovered sufficiently to insist on making the breakfast coffee," said Natasha.

"Very typical," said Pinturicchio. "My mother would have reacted just like that. The women of these parts are a wonderful lot."

"What about Giulietta?"

"She will be charged," he said. "As soon as she's in a condition to make a statement. At present, she's in the hospital under sedation. It has to be said that the women of the rising generation aren't to be compared with the Sra. Capuccis."

"She did it? She killed Guido?"

He nodded, and she saw that he had a thinning patch on the crown of his head, over which the front hair was carefully combed. "Undoubtedly," he said. "Do you have any reason to think otherwise, Miss Collingwood?"

"She may have found him."

Pinturicchio produced a pack of cigarettes, offered it to Natasha, and when she declined, lit one for himself with an air of silky voluptuousness.

"Did you know Guido?" he asked. "Did you know him well?"

She felt a flush mount to her cheeks, and despised herself for it. "You do know, don't you, that I've only been here since Wednesday?"

"That wasn't what I asked you, Miss Collingwood," he said evenly.

"No. I didn't know him well."

"But you had met him."

"Yes."

"And spoken to him."

"Yes."

"Alone."

"Yes."

Somewhere out of her vision, Sergeant Rizzio, who was leaning against the wall by the window, shifted his position slightly; his shoes squeaked.

"Would you like to tell me about that occasion, please? It was after you had interceded with some lads who were ill-using a kitten, wasn't it?"

"Yes," she said, surprised.

"For this type of information, one doesn't need to be a police-man," said Pinturicchio. "By the end of that day, everyone in the village had heard about it. I'm interested in what happened between you and Guido after the incident with the kitten."

"Nothing happened."

Pinturicchio tilted his head back and blew out a neat smoke ring.

"But you kissed."

"He kissed me." This man is trying to snare me into losing my temper, or falling about with embarrassment, she thought. But I'm not going to oblige.

"And made a proposition?"

She shrugged. "Yes."

He delicately tapped the ash from his cigarette end. "Miss Collingwood, you are a guest to my country, and the last thing I want to do is to insult you . . ." (like hell it is, she thought) ". . . but I must ask you one thing . . ."

"No. I didn't!" she said flatly.

Rizzio's shoes squeaked, and Pinturicchio looked affronted.

"Not solely on account of his age," she continued, "nor because he was my social inferior and a foreigner, or anything like that. In fact, I found him rather attractive, after his fashion . . . but I just don't happen to be an easy lay, Inspector."

(Now *he's* looking embarrassed. One in the eye for the bottom-pinching brigade!)

Pinturicchio cleared his throat, and said: "To continue. Following on this incident, you later returned to the Villa Gaspari. That evening, after Sr. Yardley had been taken to the hospital, something happened to this kitten that you had taken into your charge."

"Yes. It fell from my window and was killed."

"From the same window, was it not, from which Miss Hislop met her death last Monday night?"

"Yes."

He lit another cigarette from the stub of his first. "Tell me, Miss Collingwood. Did you ever hear about the pet dog that belonged to your predecessor?"

"Yes, I heard about it yesterday afternoon—from the Principessa di Roberti."

He drew down the corners of his lips and looked impressed. "From the *principessa,* was it? Well, now."

"Inspector!" Natasha heard her own voice take on the hard edge of irritation. "I've heard this all before—the putative link between the deaths of Susannah Hislop, her dog, and the kitten. I've thought about it a lot, and I think it's highly speculative, highly coloured, and somewhat unlikely . . ."

He held up his hand, gently silencing her.

"Miss Collingwood," he said, "just now, you expressed doubts about the probability that Giulietta killed Guido. I think I should put you further in the picture. In the first place, she and Guido were lovers; had been lovers, in the way that these things are done between the young people of these parts, from puberty. She was pregnant . . ." he glanced down at his note-pad ". . . she was five months pregnant by him, on her own admission. Last night, following their custom, no doubt, she went down to the beach to meet her lover, taking with her a blanket, for a particular purpose. That was not all she took down with her, Miss Collingwood—but more of that later.

"You will have formed your own opinion of Guido. He was a child of his time, a child of this place. Things have much improved, of recent years, in these parts, but there is nothing here for the Guidos; they make a few lire, in the summer, as beach boys; in the winter, they go hungry. The bright ones get factory jobs up in the north, or go to be waiters in London or Paris. Guido was not so bright. He stayed, and had the pick of the girls.

"He had Miss Hislop. Oh, yes, I assure you he did. It caused quite a disturbance up at the Villa Gaspari, and Mr. Yardley nearly sent her back to England. She stayed—and her dog was found drowned."

Natasha felt her scalp prickle with the shock of what he was, surely, implying. "You're trying to tell me that Giulietta killed the dog because Susannah Hislop went with her lover?" she said.

Pinturicchio hunched his shoulders and spread his hands in a fine Italian gesture of yes-no.

"Or that she killed Susannah, when she ignored the warning?"

The shrug became even more elaborate and ambiguous.

"Or even that . . ."

"I will only say this," he said, "for it would be improper for me to commit myself further at this stage: Giulietta Capucci will be charged on the evidence of having been found with her slain lover, with his blood on her hands, and with the knife with which he was killed. The knife came from the kitchen of the Villa Gaspari, to which she had easy access. It is a butcher's knife, of the type that is used to slice meat. It is small, but heavy, and very sharp in the blade. With such a knife, even a not very robust young girl could, with a wild slash to the body, take a man's life in a very terrible way. Particularly, Miss Collingwood, if her arm was directed by a frenzy of . . . jealousy?" He inflected the final word, to make it a question.

"Jealous of . . . *me* . . . you mean? But, as I told you . . ."

"You told me you had refused him. I believe you. Did you, also, reassure Giulietta Capucci that there was nothing between you and the father of her unborn child? But, come, I am being unfair. You have been here only a few days, and you are already implicated—innocently implicated—in this dreadful business, and have been upset quite enough."

Natasha was scarcely listening to him.

"It must have happened while I was with Nathan Yardley," she said, more than half to herself. "While we were waiting for the ambulance to arrive. Anyone looking up from the kitchen yard could have seen the kitten sitting on the window sill of my room . . ."

"I won't bother you any more today," said Pinturicchio, rising. "I appreciate your co-operation in coming to see me. Please don't upset yourself any further."

His eyes wavered, avoiding the stare she threw at him.

"You think I'm . . . implicated?" she demanded.

"I think it may be found that you, yourself, have had a very narrow escape, Miss Collingwood," said Pinturicchio, quietly, without looking up.

The two police officers watched her through the window: They saw her turn the corner, knotting a scarf that she had put over her head against a new flurry of rain.

"Nice-looking girl," said Sergeant Rizzio. "There's nothing quite like a tall one, you know."

"There should be more of them about," agreed his superior.

"Why did you push her so far? You really scared her."

"She's tougher than she looks, didn't you notice that? No shrinking little English miss, she. I spelled it out to her. She can take it."

"Think it will do any good, Inspector?"

"It might. If one piles on enough pressure, something will have to give," said Pinturicchio. He took out another cigarette and lit it from the stub of his second.

Violent murder in a peasant village community will always set in train a canon of behaviour that is imposed on the inhabitants by a common bond of ignorance, credulity, and poverty. This nexus determines the people's attitude to those closely involved in the murder, to the law, and to each other.

In any urban street in Europe and America, a murder will produce a crowd of mindless onlookers to the comings and goings in the house where the killing took place; and yet Natasha Collingwood was able to walk, unmolested and—seemingly—unwatched, from the *polizia* to the Villa Gaspari.

Any urban murder anywhere in the world will immediately be attended by an avalanche of interference from false witnesses, exhibitionists, ill-wishers, the death-wished, do-gooders, and other cranks; but the telephone in Aldo Pinturicchio's borrowed office in the village *polizia* remained obdurately silent.

The attitude of the accused girl's mother, the widow Maria Capucci, conformed to the rule of the community. A night of tears and breast-beating, with loud appeals to the Madonna and specific local saints for intercession, ended with the dawn and the need to carry on living. Coffee and hot rolls appeared at nine o'clock sharp in the Villa Gaspari—just like every other morning. The ethnic memory of the peasant allows only two alternatives: work or starve.

The whole village, then, went about its work. No one contacted the police with information; for the law represented —and not without justification—a mindless and capricious source of energy that could so easily upset the delicate balance of a peasant's economy (Who picks the lemons or nets the mullet, if you're being questioned all day by a sharp fellow from Naples, whose instinctive response to your gracious offer of help is to try to pin the crime on you?).

Even the unemployed men (there are no unemployed women in southern Italy) and the young *flâneurs* in their cheap groovy gear held the line against involvement. The men drank coarse wine at the café tables in the square, and played cards; the youths grouped at the street corners and on the wall at the top of the beach, whistled when the washer-girls came and bent to lay their damp, white sheets to dry on the hot sand. None of them took any special notice of the unusually heavy traffic of police cars between the village *polizia* and local headquarters in Amalfi, nor glanced more than was necessary towards the walls of the Villa Gaspari, rising, tier upon tier, from the blue water of the bay. Yet, thoughts of the murder scarcely left their minds. And so omnipresent and efficient was the grapevine that every soul in the village—those who worked and those who loafed—knew every detail of the movements of the principal actors in the tragedy.

"The English *signorina* has been called to the *polizia*," they whispered. "That Aldo has told her that she was lucky not to be thrown out of the window like the other one."

At his suggestion, Natasha lunched with Yardley in his room. His face bore traces of tiredness and pain, and his night's exertions had caused the knee to swell up alarmingly; despite that, his whole attention seemed to be directed to her wellbeing. Natasha, who had been awake all night after having witnessed a particularly gruesome corpse, and had spent a harrowing half-hour with the police that morning, was in need of any comfort that was going.

Over coffee, she said: "What upsets me is that I can hardly call anything to mind about Giulietta. She was the first person I met when I arrived at the villa, and she looked as if she'd been crying—presumably that was something to do with Guido and her pregnancy. Apart from that, she came across to me merely as a young and rather withdrawn girl who didn't speak English and who served at table. The only meaningful impression I have is of her screaming face, and somehow it doesn't connect with Giulietta. This strange lack of impression worries me, because it concerns a person who—if the inspector's right

—may have wanted to kill me; may even have planned to do it."

She had told him the details of her interview with Pinturic-chio, which had meant that—to her embarrassment—she had also had to tell him about the significant encounter with the dead youth. Yardley listened to it all without comment, nodding sympathetically and regarding her with an expression of thoughtful compassion. It struck her for the first time that he was a very good listener. As he was to show, he was also capable of exercising a perceptiveness that was almost feminine in its gentle subtlety.

"Giulietta is an unremarkable girl," he said. "Which is why you haven't formed a strong impression of her. As a writer, you unconsciously evaluate the strength and interest of people's characters. I should tell you that, from my longer acquaintance with the poor kid, I hang exactly the same labels on her: withdrawn, a face that serves at table, negligible. You're quite right, Natasha: Not till she was reacting to her killing of her lover did one ever register a strong impression of Giulietta."

"Yet—she killed," said Natasha. "Could anyone who was entirely negligible do anything so—so hideously positive?"

Yardley shook his head and laid his hand on her arm.

"Trust your writer's instinct," he said. "It gives you the clue to what murder is. You registered Giulietta as a negative personality; murder is the ultimate null. It is always committed for the basest possible reasons, mostly without premeditation or planning, ineptly, and in such a way as to ensure the eventual destruction of the murderer himself. It's an extended form of self-destruction. There's nothing positive about murder: As an artist, a creative artist, you know that in your heart."

Yardley took away his hand, and she felt a distinct sense of deprivation. She had drawn her chair close to his bedside, and he was propped up in the pillows, wearing his grey dressing gown, with an Indian silk scarf wound like a stock round his bronzed neck.

He smiled at her, and there was an impish touch of mischief in his eyes. "Get your notebook," he said. "It's suddenly come to me that I must write a note to my publishers."

Her notebook and pen were on the table by the window, together with a pile of newly arrived fan mail that she had brought to show him. A few moments later, she was sitting with her pen poised over the paper.

"Address it to Jay Stewart, the big man himself," said Yardley. "Dear Jay, the accompanying typescript is by my secretary, Natasha Collingwood . . ."

She glanced up at him and felt her cheeks glowing.

". . . who, as you will quickly discover on reading some of her material, is something quite out of the ordinary as a writer . . ."

It seemed too wonderful to be anything other than a daydream, a piece of Walter Mittyish fantasticating; but it was for real: She was actually shaping the words on the paper before her, and they were *his* words.

". . . In fact, I would go so far as to say that her short stories are the most excitingly original that I have read, in this particular genre, for many years. . . ."

It was like a homecoming; a return from the wilderness. How many tears had dried on this lost hope, now so gloriously re-awakened?

". . . Paragraph . . . If you were to make Miss Collingwood an offer for the publication of her collection of short stories, I would be happy . . . no, change that to honoured . . . I would be honoured to contribute a critical appreciation by way of an introduction.

"And that, my dear Natasha," he said, "will clinch it as far as Jay Stewart's concerned. I'm a great believer in nepotism; where would I have been without it?"

"Nathan . . ." she bowed her head and blinked her eyes, and a tear splashed on her hand . . . "this makes me so happy, I don't know where to begin to find the words to thank you."

"Dedicate the book to me. That'll give me an enormous amount of pleasure."

"Oh, of course I will."

She was groping for a handkerchief, head still bowed, when he leaned forward and, taking her gently by the shoulders, kissed her lightly on the brow. There was a knock on the door.

It was Eric.

"Sorry to barge in," he said, "but I was wondering if Natasha remembered about the religious festival this evening, and if she still wants to go."

"Oh, have a heart, old chap," said Yardley. "Natasha didn't get a wink of sleep last night after what happened. She won't want to traipse around the streets this evening. I should explain, Natasha, that the festival's one of those ghastly semi-pagan routs that only southern Latins could devise, stuffed with plaster saints, candles, and flagellants. They also have, I should admit, a quite spectacular firework display—which is the attraction as far as Eric's concerned. Sorry, old chap, but you'll have to give it a miss this year."

The boy's mouth went slack, and his blue eyes suspiciously moist.

"We'll go, Eric," said Natasha.

"You're over-indulging him. I won't have it," said Yardley, with mock severity. Eric grinned happily.

"What time does it begin?" asked Natasha.

"I've never seen the start of it," said Eric, "but the fireworks don't begin till after dark, of course. You could have a nap,

Natasha, and I'll wake you in time for an early dinner before we set off. Okay?"

"You have no choice," said Yardley.

"I'll go and have that nap, then," said Natasha. "Do you need me any more, Nathan?"

"No," he smiled at her. "But don't forget to type the letter for me to sign."

"As if I would," she said. "I'll do it straight away. And . . . thank you again for giving me this wonderful help, Nathan."

"You deserve it. And, like I always say, we artists have to stick together, for there aren't many of us left."

And that was the wonderful thing about him, she thought: Only he could have taken her—tired, depressed, and filled with a dreadful unease, as she had been before lunch—and have lifted her spirits the way they were now. He had something very special, and, surely, it was the thing they call star quality.

He was right, also, about poor little Giulietta. What was the phrase he used? Murder is an extended form of self-destruction (and, surely, that was a quote right out of *Pride Goes Before*). Giulietta had killed her lover to ensure her own destruction and the destruction of her unwanted child. That was the beginning, the middle, and the ending of it. There were the peripheral questions, of course: Had she also been responsible for Susannah's death, and the deaths of the two animals? And then, there was the defilement of Susannah's grave. . . .

Natasha decided that she was too tired to work it out. All that mattered was that no one else would be hurt, neither she nor anyone else.

Tomorrow. She'd think about it tomorrow. First, type that wonderful letter, then get some sleep.

## 9

They arrived at the place of the procession a little before sunset. It was a village with an unpronounceable name, dominated by a vast, neglected-looking church in a dusty square; the rest of the square was made up of tall tenement houses, from whose windows issued lines of washing and—from some —the slam of pop music and the limelit green glare of television screens. An evening wind blew powdery dust in ghostly eddies across the cobblestones, and Natasha, who wished she had brought a sweater, shivered and hugged herself in an uncomfortable metal seat at an outside café table.

She and Eric were the only clientele of the café; indeed, they were the only people in the square—though, from time to time, faces appeared at tenement windows and looked down at them speculatively, sometimes summoning other faces to regard them.

An old man in a seedy gown—a sacristan or a verger—scurried into the square and up the steps of the church; the great door banged behind him, reverberating hollowly in unseen recesses.

"Why did that chap glare at us like that?" asked Eric, nervously.

"Wondering what in heaven's name we're doing here, I shouldn't wonder," said Natasha. Sleep had refreshed her to the point where a quiet evening with a book, or letter writing (and wouldn't Veronica *writhe* with envy, to hear that she was going to be published?) would have been an agreeable way of ending the day; the present activity was already going bad.

"You don't think we've come on the wrong evening?" faltered Eric; and the treacherous moistness was already glazing his susceptible eyes. "I'm sure it happens tonight. Look. They've got the decorations up." He pointed to a line of tired-looking pennants strung between lamp-posts.

"We'll just have to wait and see, won't we, darling?" said Natasha. And added, placatingly: "Even if it isn't tonight, the climb up to here was an absolute revelation, and well worth repeating tomorrow. Such views!"

Backward-glancing views across the gulf, and along the coast of the peninsula as far as Capri, hard-edged against the sinking sun, had, indeed, been spectacular; but the final part of the ascent—by a stone-cut stairway that snaked up the almost-sheer face of the peak on whose crest the village stood —had been so vertiginous that Natasha had associated it with looking down from an aircraft. She shuddered at the memory of it. The village itself, set on its narrow shelf, was surely in constant hazard, she thought. The square, with its high, enclosing walls of church and tenements, looked safe enough; but a few steps down any of the alleyways leading off the square brought one to the edge of destruction; and the rear of some of the tenements almost overhung the abyss. Shudder again.

"I need a drink," she said. "Where's that boy?" She had ordered a brandy and dry ginger for her and a natural lemonade for Eric from a squint-eyed youth who had long since disappeared into the dark archway of the café door. "Come to think of it, we can ask him if we've got the right night for the festival—if he ever comes back again."

"I feel rather hungry," said Eric. He had recovered from

the small attack of dejection, and was surreptitiously dabbing the corners of his eyes with the tip of his little finger and wiping the moistness onto his trousers. "Do you suppose they'll have sandwiches, Natasha?"

"You should have eaten your dinner," said Natasha. "All you did was push your meat around the plate and spear a few beans."

"I hate meat," he said. "And, besides, I was rather too excited to eat then."

From one of the high campaniles that flanked the façade of the church, the thin, flat note of a bell began to sound a rapid peal. *Nang-nang-nang-nang-nang.* It was like a summons.

"Perhaps the festival's going to begin now," said Eric.

The street lamps came on, and, in the act of bringing a new degree of illumination to the shadowy square, they made a clear-cut division between day and night. Before them, all was day; now it was night. And, curiously, warmer. The wind died, and the dust clouds settled.

*Nang-nang-nang-nang-nang* . . .

"Everything's changed!" breathed Eric.

"Yes! Yes!"

In the lamplight, the night zephyrs now grandly stirred the mean pennants in folds of velvety plum and rich blue; beyond the lamplight, the high façades of the tenements took on a sudden nobility of outline. The lines of washing had, by a deft piece of unseen stage management, all been snatched away. And the great church loomed blackly over everything.

A man and a woman came out of the café and began to fold up the metal chairs and tables, to carry them away and provide more open space in the square. The squint-eyed youth, who had taken their order and neglected to do anything about it, lifted down a red-white-and-green Cinzano sign and put it out of sight. The man approached them, and bowed apologetically to Natasha. She stood up.

"What about our drinks?" asked Eric.

"You can forget them," said Natasha. "Likewise your sandwiches. The big show is definitely about to begin."

From every alleyway and door, people were filing into the square and massing against the walls, leaving an open space in the centre. Natasha took Eric's hand, and they went to stand by the café entrance. She noticed that most of the women were in black, and all wore veils over their heads, as if in church; and she blessed the impulse that had made her bring a silk scarf.

An air of expectancy hung over the lamp-encircled square, over the dark church, and Natasha sensed that a strangeness was about to visit the lonely village on the hilltop. There was a murmuring among the people; they were praying, some of them kneeling with their rosaries. The solitary bell continued its tolling, high above the lamplight, where the night sky was now quite dark.

"I'm scared," whispered Eric in her ear. "Aren't you scared, too, Natasha?"

"Scared of what?" asked Natasha, ruefully aware that he had probed for, and found, a weakness in her. She was, indeed, full of a nameless unease—had been so from the moment that the street lamps had killed the last of the daylight.

He squeezed her elbow. "Look!"

A line of bobbing lights—for all the world like the lights on the fishing boats that plied in the gulf—appeared in the distance, at the far end of one of the dark streets that ran along the side of the church. They were approaching from afar, very slowly—insubstantially borne, as though by wind or water, though their jiggling movements related to human gait.

The procession . . .

The bell stopped, and the doors of the church swung open, revealing a darkened sweep of nave with a candle-blaze at the far end that all but occluded a silhouetted group that stepped out and took up position in the entrance to the church. Natasha could just make out a priest in purple vestments, surrounded by a cloud of white-garbed acolytes bearing candles, censers, and tall crosses.

"Oh, blast!" growled Eric. "Amanda and her lot have turned up. That's ditched everything."

"Wheeee! Hi! Hi, Miss Collingwood, baby!" The voice of the not-so-boyish Bimbo with the Afro hair-do. They were on the opposite side of the square—six of them, in all their expensive hip gear from Rome and Paris, elbowing their ways through the sombrely dressed village people, like birds of paradise pecking among crows. Bimbo was waving, and Natasha picked out Amanda, who looked pale and angry-faced under the light of one of the lamps.

"They must have come up by road, in cars," whispered Eric. "I bet they're all either frightfully drunk, or they've been smoking pot. What a rotten bunch of outsiders. Whatever do the villagers think of them? Hope they don't come over here. Let's get away, Natasha—move to the other end of the square, away from them."

"We'd never get through all these people," said Natasha. She saw Bimbo addressing Amanda and pointing in her direction; and she remembered how the girl had reacted to her—Natasha's—first encounter with the demonstrative Bimbo.

Another bell—this time from the campanile at the other side of the church's façade—started to toll in a slow, reverberating bass.

The bobbing lights were much nearer now. In the loom of every candle's flame, she could pick out the ghost of a face; and there were men's voices raised in unison with a plainsong

dirge. Moments later, the head of the procession broke out
of the gloom of the side-street and into the square.

First came men in plain, dark suits, carrying long candle-
sticks. They wore dignified hats, and medals of old wars on
their lapels: middle-aged and elderly men, men of substance
who carried themselves proudly: the village bourgeoisie and
lay officers of the church—there were about twenty of them, in
four columns. They led the way, straight across the square and
past where Natasha and Eric stood. They did not look towards
the crowd; no searching for faces of family and friends; under
the candlelight, their shaded eyes remained resolutely to the
front.

Then came pale, tonsured friars. Some of them were very
young, and many of them extraordinarily good-looking. Under
the lights, their jowls and mouths showed the stubble in strong
tones of green and blue. It was they who bore the burden
of the plainsong dirge: The rolling Latin phrases, deeply in-
toned, had the hard masculinity of a warriors' lament for the
fallen. Unlike the worthies in the dignified hats, they looked
freely about them as they walked slowly past the watching
faces; they were altogether more assured, grave saunterers in
grey and brown.

"Here comes the first of the local saints," whispered Eric. "I
don't know his name, but bits of his bones are made up into
the statue. The flagellants come after the saints. I shall look
away then—I can't bear that sort of thing."

"I think I shall, too," said Natasha, feelingly.

The first statue was borne on the backs of sweating men,
toiling under the weight of the long poles supporting the
throne on which sat a wax representation of an old man in
bishop's robes—real robes, brocaded, jewel-encrusted. The
figure's eyes were of glass, and the long teeth looked real. One
of the bearers let out a groan of protest, and others came for-

ward with short, thick poles, which they placed under the throne. The bearers were able to straighten up and spit on their hands. The procession faltered; halted for a while; then the men took up their burden and continued on their way.

They went by, one by one, swaying on tired shoulders: saints and martyrs with waxen cheeks and painted tears, looking out with unseeing dolly eyes over the worshipping crowd, who knelt and genuflected at their passing. The last of the statues was that of a young girl in white, whose appearance brought groans and sobs from the women. By this time, the friars' dirge was no more than a deep murmur at the far end of the square; another sound was taking over—a quite different sound.

Eric clutched again at Natasha's elbow. "I shall stop watching now," he said. "Tell me when they've gone past. Well past." He turned his head away, laying his cheek against her upper arm; she felt the downy softness of his unshaven skin.

They came in single file, behind the statue of the little virgin-martyr: young men in tattered gowns reaching to their ankles. They moved in a zig-zag line, snaking along the processional route, from one edge of the crowd to the other. Each man carried some sort of whip, and, with every step, each brought his whip with swinging violence over his shoulder and across his back. The sound was like heavy rain on still water.

Natasha remembered Yardley's phrase about "ghastly semi-pagan routs," and resolved neither to be revolted nor impressed by the spectacle of the penitents and their archaic rite. In any event, she thought, the whole thing's symbolic and not for real: Penitents haven't scourged themselves for real in Europe since the Middle Ages. This is just pretend.

The leader of the snaking file demolished her comfortable

preconception with one glance of his wild eyes. His scourge was made of a bunch of electrical cables, the ends of the wires stripped of their insulation and each wire individually knotted. He came quite close to her, and mouthed something at her, as he brought the terrible implement round and over his shoulder. As the ends of the scourge whined past in its arc, she felt a splattering, as of light rain, on one hand and arm. Next moment, the man had turned to make the next leg of his zig-zag—and she saw the state of his back. It was scored in deep weals, as if by a butcher's knife, and running red.

Sickened and suddenly faint, she lowered her eyes—and saw that her own hand and arm had been spattered by his blood.

"Let's get out of here, Eric," she said.

But there was no way out. The area by the café doorway, where they were standing, was now a solid wedge of people in a state of crowd ecstasy, who pressed them ever closer to the processional route. She put an arm round Eric, who still had his face held against her. His shoulders were trembling.

"Please! Please let us pass." She felt her voice taking on an edge of panic. The people were now moaning and crying aloud with each fall of the cruel whips. No one could hear her; no one was listening. They stood together, alone in a sea of kneeling zealots. Somewhere up in the night, a chorus of bells was adding its wild clamour to the din. Natasha closed her eyes and willed for time to pass, holding the trembling boy close to her, her skin crawling against the contact of the splattering droplets of blood, her ears filled with the hideous sound of the whips.

The pattern of noise and movement changed, and this meant that the procession had gone past. She opened her eyes. The crowd was moving now, surging to follow in the wake of the penitents, and she and Eric were being carried along with them. Not that—not at any price.

Still holding the boy, she elbowed someone aside—and came face to grinning face with Bimbo. He held her, as they swayed together in the crowd.

"Hi, again, Miss Collingwood, baby. My, you look like some cat scared the pretty pants right off you, ain't that right, Mandy-baby?"

Amanda was at his elbow. In a solid wedge behind him were the other four. One of them was a girl in green, demon-queen sun-glasses who was smoking a long cigar. Amanda looked furious, and it was all directed, for some reason, at Eric.

"What are you doing here, for heaven's sake? You should be in bed. Christ, you look washed-out!"

"Nathan said it was alright for Natasha to bring me," whined her brother.

Amanda's eyes flickered resentfully towards Natasha—who felt a wave of dislike that was almost tactile. "Well, it's time you went home now," she said. "Bimbo, will you take us back to the villa."

"Not till the fireworks are over!" wailed Eric. "I only came for the fireworks, and they start in a minute."

"Shut up, you little fool!" blazed his sister. "Bimbo, will you take us home?"

The epicine Bimbo was in no mood for obedience. He grinned playfully. "Why, the party's only just got started, Mandy-baby. Whyfore you want to break up this good scene, huh?" He swayed aside, indulgently, to let a fat woman squirm past him. "What do the rest of you cats say to that? There's food for the soul in this scene. Let's catch it."

The group of them was now an island in an advancing sea of people. The square was emptying after the procession, which had become again a line of bobbing lights at the end of another narrow street beyond. Natasha was no longer holding

Eric. It seemed to her that all she had to do was to stand still, and let the crowds wash past her, leaving her alone in the empty square. But, even as she examined the concept, the press of people became impossible to withstand; she was edged along, against her will and resistance. And then Bimbo was beside her: His arm was round her waist, his breathy voice close to her ear.

"Relax and drift with it, baby. Come on. Let's go."

"No—please!" she protested.

It was no use. He was going with the stream and taking her along with him. There were ecstatic faces close around her, eyes glazed, and lips moving in prayer. Her captor was holding her tightly against his lean flanks, arm still imprisoning her waist. The pressure of bodies all round her made it impossible to raise her own arms and break free of his grasp; and, even if she had been able to do that, the sheer pressure of the crowd would have kept them in the same contiguousness.

They drifted out of the lamplit square and into the darkness of the high-walled street beyond. The forcing of the crowd into the narrow funnel of the street further compressed the squirming mass of sweating bodies. Somewhere close at hand, a woman screamed. Bimbo's mouth was doing something moist and intimate with the side of Natasha's neck, and there was no preventing him. She tried to will herself into a state of mental withdrawal, but the physical sensations of heat, intolerable pressure, and the difficulty of breathing precluded anything like that.

There was a spluttering and a cannonading in the sky, and they moved from blackness into an artificial daylight of such sudden whiteness as to reveal minute texture of stonework, hair, and skin. Another thunder-clap, and a star tore itself apart and scattered in a thousand fiery tails above the street. By its great light, she saw the Afro-capped head above her, monstrously large, as his mouth came down towards her.

"Relax, baby. Relax. This is real soul-food. Drift with it."

The fireworks were continuous, and seemed to have been going on forever. Sight and hearing were dulled and flattened by the assault.

Somewhere along the street, she had blessedly lost Bimbo. The advancing tail of the procession—of which they were a part—had been joined, at an intersection, by a fresh influx of people from both sides. Three advancing streams, fusing into one, had caused disruptions to the dynamics of the crowd, and in one of these violent movements, she and the hedonistic Bimbo had been wrenched apart. Blessedly.

She was now in the middle of the street, still hemmed in on all sides, and being carried along in the power of the procession. The fireworks' glare showed the end of the street close ahead, and with it the end of the village. With a sudden lurch of the heart, Natasha remembered the sheer drop that lay beyond the farthest tenement buildings. The thought reminded her of her responsibility towards her young charge. Where was Eric? He had to be somewhere in the procession; he could never have broken free of it.

She called aloud: "Eric! Eric, can you hear me?"

A fresh ripple of explosions drowned her cries.

"Eric!" she called again.

As the press of bodies drew near the end of the street, there was a quickening of movement in the centre of the stream, and those who were slower or more reluctant—like Natasha—were sloughed off towards the outer edges. She had a wild hope, to reach the haven of a doorway, where she could break free.

The last doorway went past, with two people between her and escape. Next instant, she was on the outside of the crowd, and still being carried along, but now the mass had changed direction—a swirling, curved movement in whose vortex she was driven by the pressure of those behind her.

And there was no escape to the side. The procession had turned a corner at the end of the street, and was now circling the perimeter of the village on the high peak.

She shrank nearer to the edge of the crowd, now, the way a child clings to a spinning roundabout in a playground, lest the force of its turning should cast him off and throw him clear.

Now the attachment to the rapidly turning vortex was her only protection—her only protection from whatever lay beyond a low stone wall that lined the cobbled road on the edge of the village. And a splutter of rocketry out above the abyss showed her what lay beyond: There was a sheer drop into an unimaginable depth; she heard the echoes of the explosions reverberate among the vineyards and lemon groves far below.

And she was being inexorably edged towards the low wall.

She held onto the shoulder of a man ahead of her, but a sideways motion of the crowd dragged him away. She turned her back to the crowd, facing the wall, bracing herself against the people behind her.

Somewhere out there in the night, by a simple exercise of hideous imagination, she pictured the gulf and the coastal plain and headlands as far as Capri—all waiting to receive her falling body, toppling to doom in a vertiginous nightmare.

All of which was ridiculous. Already, the curving movement was beginning to straighten out, and the pressure on her back was slackening. She was very close to the wall now: It was just beyond her touch, and the top of it was perilously low, barely reaching above her knees. It needed, she thought, another few courses of stonework, like the window sill in Susannah's bedroom, now her bedroom. . . .

But it was going to be all right. The pressure had gone. She would be forced no nearer to the wall.

It was then that she felt the palm of an unseen hand being placed—quite deliberately—against the small of her back. A jerking push, directed with all the power in an unseen body—and she was hurled against the wall, knees striking it, the upper part of her body already overbalanced and a scream of mortal horror leaping to her lips.

She was half over the edge—poised in a timeless instant in all eternity, helpless as a puppet with broken strings, her balance quite irrecoverable—when her left ankle was taken in a powerful double grip. A rocket exploded overhead, and she saw the valley beneath the peak—every rock and treetop waiting to receive her—before she was hauled back to safety and unceremoniously dumped on the ground with her back against the wall. Then her rescuer took hold of her neck and thrust her head between her knees.

"Take some deep breaths, and throw up if you feel like it." It was a growling voice, flatly accented.

When Natasha was sufficiently recovered as to be able to look up, she saw that it was, indeed, the painter Robert Ballard who had snatched her from death.

The procession had gone by. A few coloured rockets spluttered in the sky above the church, and ended in falling specks of dying flame. From somewhere in the village came the tinny sound of a brass band playing an operatic overture. Natasha shivered.

Ballard helped her up and, taking off his jacket, laid it across her shoulders.

"I'll take you home," he said.

She went with him, meekly, her senses numb. He walked slightly in advance of her, hands sunk into his trousers pockets, head bowed, and it seemed to her that he looked like a big, sullen, marmalade-coloured bear. He led the way along the empty, dark street, till they came to an open space behind the church, where a few groups of people were gathered about parked cars. Natasha recognised three members of Amanda's high-toned hippy set standing beside a yellow Ferrari. The girl in the green sun-glasses gave her a disinterested glance as they came up.

"What happened to Eric?" asked Natasha. "Have you seen him?"

"Yeah. Bimbo drove him home just now. With Amanda . . ." She turned her back on Natasha and addressed her companions: "This place died. I'm screaming for a joint. Why don't we go some place else? Like Positano."

Ballard had unlocked the door of a battered VW beetle and was holding it open for her, though his reflective eyes never left the group by the Ferrari. "Hop in," he murmured, gruffly.

She obeyed. They drove down the dark road by the side of the church and into the main square. It looked quite different, now. The café tables were crowded, and the Cinzano sign was back. What appeared to be the town band was grouped on the church steps. They were playing—with sketchy attention to harmony and tempo—a lively tarantella, and a few couples were whirling together under the lamplight. The unearthly procession might never have been; it was any southern Italian village on the night of a *festa*.

There was a group of young men standing together near the café entrance. Some of them wore flat caps, and all had jackets over tattered gowns that reached down to their ankles. With a crawling sense of horror, Natasha realised that they must be the penitents. They were laughing together, puffing cigarettes, and passing a wine bottle between them. As the

VW went past, the man with the bottle raised it in salutation to the girl inside, and shouted a cheerful obscenity.

The village was soon behind them, and Ballard was negotiating the hairpin bends of the mountainous road that led down to the coast, not stopping till they came upon a lighted café-restaurant at the top of a beach. When the little car's engine was silent, the whirring of cicadas and the sound of the waves on the shore took over.

"You look terrible," he told Natasha. "Come on. I'll buy you a stiff brandy, to liven you up."

## 10

They sat at a table on a glass-screened verandah overlooking the shadowy beach; and they were the only people in the place. The proprietress—a plump body in black bombazine—treated them with roguish archness that implied that she thought them to be lovers, and probably illicit lovers at that. She served them with drinks, and vanished through a door behind the bar, with a wink for Natasha.

"I never said thank you for what you did," said Natasha.

He shrugged his big shoulders and took a long pull at his drink.

"Thank you all the same," she said. "And I know you don't like me."

"Do you like me?"

"Does it matter to you?"

He shook his head, and the corners of his grey eyes crinkled with sudden amusement. It was the first time she had seen Ballard register anything approaching good humour.

"How's the *principessa?*" she asked.

"Sprightly as ever. Still devotedly interested in things that go on about her."

"You mean—in other people's business."

"You could put it that way," he said. "It's a classic pastime of the elderly. You could get around to it yourself one day—if you survive to grow old, that is," he added, flatly.

Natasha looked down at her hands, and was conscious for

the first time that they were trembling; had probably been trembling since the time of the procession.

In a small voice, she said: "Someone deliberately tried to push me over that wall, did you know?"

Some moments went by before he replied: "I didn't know. I looked round and saw you going, that's all. No, I didn't know someone pushed you."

"Are you surprised to hear it?"

He shrugged.

"You're not very communicative, are you?" she said. "But will you tell me one thing?"

"Try me."

"Why that grotesque tea-party? Why was that staged, to interrogate me? What were you and the *principessa* hoping to find out from me?"

Ballard drained his glass, and wiped his lips on a white-spotted red handkerchief. "It was the old lady's idea," he said. "She learned that morning, on the village grape-vine, about your cat having fallen to its death the previous evening. She telephoned me right away; told me to come round for tea, to meet you, and to help her."

"Help her? To grill me?"

"It wasn't a grilling," he said. "We were trying to warn you."

"Warn me?"

There was no need for him to say anything else. The state of her hands were the give-away: the hands of a person in mortal fear of death; the hands of someone who lately gazed over the abyss, and whose dreams would be forever haunted by what she had seen there.

"Someone's trying to kill me. You think that, don't you? You and the *principessa* think that, which is why the tea-party took the course it did yesterday. But who is it that's trying to kill me? Who? Do you know?"

He shook his head. "I don't say someone's trying to kill you. I say that you're in a bad situation, and if you don't know what I mean by that, maybe me and the *principessa* stuck our necks out for nothing. But all I can say is this . . ."

"Yes?"

He looked down into his empty glass for a while before replying: It was as if he had the words framed quite clearly in his mind, but was doubtful of the propriety of uttering them. His eyes, when he looked up again, were guarded and wary.

"Events have shown—and I include whatever it was that nearly happened to you up there tonight . . ." he gestured up towards the mountain, away from the sea ". . . that you are being menaced in much the same way that your lady predecessor was menaced before she came to her end. And if you say you don't know why, well then, either you were born yesterday, or you must think I was born yesterday."

(Again, she was back in Pinturicchio's makeshift office in the village *polizia* that morning, with the paunchy inspector avoiding her eyes and delicately tapping his ash; the squeak of the policeman's shoes . . .

*"Miss Collingwood . . . the last thing I want to do is to insult you . . . but I must ask you one thing . . ."*)

Natasha got to her feet. He remained seated, looking up at her with the same reflective, flat stare he had given Amanda's friends.

"Thank you for the drink," she said. "And for the gratuitous insult you just can't bring yourself to spell out in straight talk."

"You want it," said Ballard. "Here it is. In the time she was here, Susannah Hislop went close to turning this village on its ear. I don't know if Yardley's given you any idea of her proclivities, but I can tell you that he couldn't have exaggerated. I think she died because of that, and I'll take bets that I'm found to be correct, whether they nail the actual killing onto little Giulietta or onto someone else. Susannah was warned, but she didn't take the warnings. She stayed—and came to a bad end.

"In round terms—spelt out in the kind of straight talk you've been asking for—Susannah Hislop died because she was the worst kind of whore.

"What kind of whore are you, Miss Collingwood?"

The Villa Gaspari was less than a mile along the coast road: she saw the familiar configuration of its white buildings at the other side of a small bay as soon as she walked out of the café-restaurant. There was plenty of traffic on the road to light her way.

Natasha had already been at the door of the bar by the time Ballard had delivered his penultimate remark. The sheer brutality of his final question had made her rest her hand against the wall, to steady herself. But she had resisted going back and slapping his face, or making a Parthian shot, or anything like that. It has its drawbacks, but a happy rural upbringing, in genteel, though impoverished family circumstances, gives a girl the stability and assurance to withdraw from a situation.

Her only fear was that Robert Ballard would come after her; cruise along beside her, perhaps, and try to apologise. In the event, she need have had no such trepidations: Soon she was knocking on the gate of the villa. Old Mario came up and let her in, mumbled good night, and went back to the kitchen quarters.

Natasha knew what she had to do. It still wanted a quarter of an hour till eleven, and Nathan Yardley would almost certainly still be awake. Then, if awake, she would settle things with him tonight—the things she had resolved in her mind during the walk along the coast road.

Her eyes, staring back at her from the mirror, looked over-large and theatrical; and that wasn't bad, because she could scarcely remember a time when her hair had looked so mousey, or her nose so prominent and aggressive.

She was angry, she decided—and that wasn't bad, either. Full marks to Ballard—that dauber, that peasant—for finding her full of mortal fear, and leaving her seething with righteous fury.

A few moments later, she was tapping gently.

"Who is it?"

"It's Natasha. Can I see you for a few moments, please, Nathan?"

"Sure. Just a second, will you, my dear."

And then: "Come in."

He was lying in bed, as before. As she came in, he took off a pair of half-moon glasses and laid them on the bedside table, along with a thick notebook bound in green leather, with his initials on the cover.

"Have a nice evening, the two of you?" he asked. "I've been doing some work on the new book. Did I say new book? I must have written a thousand words of notes since you went out, but none of it's ever going to come to anything. I lie, I do myself less than justice—it might distil down to a telling half-paragraph. The artist's life . . ." he stared at her ". . . I say, what's the matter?"

She took a deep breath, and said: "Nathan, I'm terribly sorry. I think the terms of the agency leave me with an obligation to serve a month's notice and to refund the cost of my air ticket if I leave of my own accord within three months. Well, I'll happily pay you for the ticket, but . . ."

"Why?" he demanded. "Why?"

She avoided his gaze. "I'm asking you to relieve me from having to serve out my notice. After all, you don't really need me at the moment. There's only the fan-mail, and . . ."

"Sit down," he said. "Over there, in the button-back chair by the window, so I can see you. And just tell me all."

She obeyed.

"It's this rotten business of the deaths, isn't it?" he demanded. "First Susannah, and now that poor child Giulietta and her tragedy. I'm not surprised that you want to leave; a person with less courage and integrity would have been back home in England already. But, now, suddenly you want to go immediately. Tomorrow, I suppose. Can I ask why?"

She was prompted—it had been her specific intention—to tell him of Ballard's insinuations. Now something was stopping her. She looked down at her hands: no longer trembling, but still unsteady; curiously not her own any longer.

"I hadn't felt myself involved in it—only objectively, like watching a play—till this evening," she said. "Now, on thinking it over, I realise that I am involved, have become progressively more and more involved."

"So you want out?"

"Yes, Nathan. Before it gets—any worse."

"Look, Natasha," he said. "It's over. That poor kid's going to be tried for the murder of her lover. That's bad—but the cloud's gone away, Natasha. The sun's going to shine tomorrow over this place."

She got up and crossed over to the window. The fishing boats had either returned to the beach or were too far out in the gulf to be seen.

"In the crowd tonight, during the procession, I think someone deliberately tried to push me over a low wall," she said. "I could have been killed."

"No!" His voice was shocked, incredulous.

"I may be mistaken," she said. "I admit that, at the time, I was in a scared and nervy state. Practically hysterical. I'm a bit claustrophobic in crowds, you see. Always have been."

"Then that's the answer," said Yardley. "Whatever reason would anyone have to do that to *you?* Why, you've only been here four days. You've scarcely met anyone or done anything."

She turned back to face him. The bone structure of his lean face seemed more prominent than usual. He seemed older, more—vulnerable. She felt her resolve beginning to fray at the edges, and thought of the thick notebook with its night of useless work.

"Don't go," he said. "Don't chuck the whole thing up on account of having had a bad scare tonight—for a scare's all it was, I promise you. Who, in this part of the world, could possibly wish you any harm?"

(*"What kind of whore are you, Miss Collingwood?"*)

"There's more to it than that," she began.

"There's no more to it than that. Natasha, I'll lay it on the line. I need you. As of this living moment, in my work situation and in my life, I'm like a ship without a rudder. All this . . ." he made a hopeless gesture towards the green notebook ". . . the nagging fear that, after all, I'm only a one-book man. It's not just a private secretary I need here, Natasha, it's someone with sympathy and intelligence from whom I can bounce ideas . . . impressions. What help do you suppose I get from the children? Amanda and I don't exist in the same world. Eric—well—one does get a little weary of shoring-up the poor lad's frantic, but quite fruitless, ambitions to compensate for his academic shortcomings by becoming a cricket star . . ."

He grinned at her. It was the sudden, unexpected, self-deprecating grin that had served him so well in "As Me Another"; the gesture that had disarmed his opponents and charmed a watching nation.

"Don't go, Natasha. I need you. Without you around, there could very well never be another best seller."

So she agreed to stay. And, on the way up to her own room,

she carried two very strong impressions in her mind. First, she hadn't told him of Ballard's insinuations because—and she was able frankly to admit it to herself—she hadn't wanted Nathan Yardley to think the slightest ill of her, which was very significant. Second, in his successful attempt to persuade her to stay at the Villa Gaspari, he hadn't invoked the help he had given her, and could continue to give her, in her writing career. And that was nice.

Feeling much better than she would have believed possible half an hour before, she opened the door of her room and went in.

The light was still on, which was to be expected. But there was a strange scent—not her own, but something aromatic and Oriental-smelling, like sandalwood—pervading the bedroom.

She heard a rustle in the bathroom beyond, and she called out.

"Who's there? Is that you, Maria?" But, surely, old Maria or her other daughter (or, lately, Giulietta) did the cleaning in the morning.

Natasha walked through into the bathroom. Amanda was standing by the wash-basin, hands behind her back, facing the newcomer with an expression of mingled fear and defiance. She was in a short nightdress that showed off her long, coltish legs, and the youthful structure of her small bosom, rising and falling with the rapidity of her laboured breathing. Her bare feet—absurd how one notices such things—were none too clean.

"What are you doing in here, Amanda?" And, when the other made a movement behind her back: "What have you got there—what are you hiding from me?"

"Go away, you bitch! Don't come near me!" hissed the girl.

Natasha had a delayed-action impression of something she had noticed during her swift progress across the bedroom.

Turning, she walked back the few paces to the door and checked on that impression: the top drawer of the chest of drawers—the one containing her smaller personal belongings like her passport, letters, bits of jewellery, and so forth—was open.

She turned back to the girl. Amanda was watching her from behind a fallen switch of long, blond hair. Slack-mouthed. Still defiant and angry—and something else.

"Just give me back what you've taken from my drawer, Amanda, and then we'll both go to bed and forget the whole thing." There didn't seem any point in using anything but sweet reasonableness. And, by way of offering her a get-out: "Were you looking for a cigarette? I don't smoke."

"Bitch!"

"Now, look here, Amanda . . ."

A sudden flaring of the girl's blue eyes gave warning, and Natasha was half-ready for her when she darted for the door, and side-stepped to meet her. They collided on the threshold, and Natasha grabbed at the other's shoulder and felt the material of the nightdress rip between her fingers. Amanda spun round and, half-falling, reached out to support herself against the door frame.

Something showered from her open hand and fell at Natasha's feet: torn shreds of stiff paper, some white, some coloured, some monochrome. Ripped-up photographs.

"Why! These are mine! Why did you take them and tear them up?"

The girl made no move when Natasha crouched and picked up the pieces. Beyond the focus of her vision, she saw, still, the long legs beneath the hem of the short nightdress. But this was all afar, and beyond the range of her consciousness, which was being suddenly affronted by, and trying unsuccessfully to come to terms with, the horror that she was holding in her fingers.

The pieces made up three snapshots, and they had been taken from a pouch in the opened drawer. Two were in colour; one in black-and-white. Each had been ripped one across and across again, and she had no difficulty in reassembling them in her two hands. The black-and-white was a picture that had been taken of Veronica and herself, by an undergraduate friend, while on a visit to Cambridge the previous spring. The colour pictures were half-lengths of herself in costume for a Christmas fancy dress ball, that she had kept for a giggle.

The horror was that, in all three of the photographs, her own eyes had been burnt out, as if by a lighted cigarette end.

Just like the dead Susannah Hislop's eyes, in the snapshot on her violated grave.

In her dream—before she woke up, sweating and apprehensive—her dragging feet were taking her back up to the cemetery at the top of the stepped cleft in the hillside. The cicadas were silent in the darkness, and only her own loud footfalls—which she tried without success to moderate—broke in upon the dreadful stillness. Betraying her.

The iron gates creaked open at her approach, moved by unseen hands. At the very threshold, she summoned all her will to turn back, or to awaken herself (for she knew it was a dream), but it was no use; she was committed to a charade, a strange *entr'acte* between night and the unborn day.

The walled amphitheatre was lit by moonlight: white graves and mausoleums, and the whispering cypresses. Her eyes, which lingered on everything within their vision, were inexorably dragged towards the fresh grave that belonged to Susannah Hislop. She was halted before it, and turned to face it.

A voice in her ear told her that tonight the dead would rise from their tombs for a short while.

She did not have long to wait. Presently, she saw the dead sitting up in their tombs, and then stepping down onto the ground. They walked about, neither looking nor talking to each other, nor to her.

She saw that Susannah Hislop was one of the risen, and she was not frightened of her, though the other's face was shrouded, concealing her expression. It seemed that Susannah might stop to talk to her, and indeed this was so. When some of her companions were already slowly climbing back into their tombs, Susannah stopped and addressed her. She said that they were much in sympathy, and that she—Susannah—would like to help her. But there was so little time, she said. Would Natasha come back to this place in about a week, and she would rise again for a short while, for the purpose, only, of helping her?

Then Natasha saw the face under the shadowy fold of the shroud, and saw that it was ashen and strained with pain. Then Susannah lay on the ground and writhed in pain. And her companions called out to her from their tombs, telling her to return, because her time was up.

There was no longer any question of contact between them. Susannah could no longer hear her voice, so great was her agony. It was only with the greatest effort that she was able to drag herself to her grave and crawl inside.

When the graveyard was still again, when the tombs were all closed, and only the cypresses moved, the voice in her ear, in answer to her puzzled question, told her that the dead suffer terribly from the causes that killed them. After much rest and recuperation, they were often able to rise up and walk about for a few moments. But that was all of it; to speak or to make any contact with the living swiftly drained away their exiguous resources. That was all there was to death, said the voice.

She knew then that there was no question of seeing Susannah again and learning the truth. The willingness to help was there, but the effort was quite beyond her power. Further to impose on her would be to subject her to agonies beyond the compass of living experience—the agonies that had already killed her.

Natasha woke with a feeling of hopelessness—with the certainty that the new day would bring new horrors, and fresh questions for which there would be no answers.

The shower was a heartening re-introduction to the world of the living; hope hardened with the puckering of her skin under the tangy coolness of the droplets' assaults. But there had to be answers to it all.

Drying herself, she went back over the aftermath of the hideous discovery of the mutilated snapshots. Far from denying everything, Amanda had brushed aside the whole matter of her intrusion. Stunned to silence, Natasha had only stared, while the near-nude, grubby, over-scented young blonde had reviled her.

"But why did you do it, Amanda? Why?" she had finally got out.

That brought only fresh vituperation. The girl was all but incoherent, and entirely disinterested in answering questions; what she had said—haltingly, screamingly, slack-mouthed and with spittle running down her chin—was that Natasha was a creature who never should be allowed to live; Natasha, she implied, was a whore beside whom the Whore of Babylon was a simple maiden in her flower.

"Unbelievable. It was unbelievable!" Natasha addressed herself aloud, as she often did, in her mirror.

In the event, convinced that narcosis—by LSD, cannabis, or

whatever was the going thing with Bimbo and the rest of Amanda's crowd—was the cause of the girl's irrational behaviour, Natasha had bundled her out into the night, and locked her bedroom door against any possible further intrusion. The defiled photographs she had flushed down the lavatory.

It was full dawn. Below her window, the statues on the lowest tier of the Villa Gaspari gesticulated towards a sea of illimitable blueness and stillness. It was incongruous that there should be so much peace in all the world—particularly in the surroundings of the Villa Gaspari.

Dragging a brush through her hair, Natasha let herself come to grips with the larger question that emerged from her spoiled photographs. . . .

If, in her inexplicable hatred, Amanda had been capable of doing this to her, would she not have been equally capable of the defilement of Susannah Hislop's grave—a defilement that had included a similar mutilation of eyes in a photograph?

And, allowing that, what else was she capable of?

It was a line of thought that led to a lot of nasty byways.

## 11

Exactly at eight o'clock—a toneless bell down in the village church was telling the hour, and Natasha was just giving a thought to the problem of getting herself a cup of coffee without running the risk of another confrontation with Amanda —there came a knock on the outer gate—a knock so tentative and withdrawn as to be half an apology for making the noise. Nevertheless, they heard it down in the kitchen quarters: Natasha saw old Mario beginning his long climb up the steps, and called out to him not to bother, but that she would answer it. Despite the timidity of the knock, she had hopes that it was the postman with, perhaps, a letter from any or all of her siblings.

The lad who delivered the mail was there, but it was the *principessa's* man Willem who had knocked. He was still wearing revealing string singlet and shorts—possibly the same ones, for they were decidedly grubby. The pink-lit albino eyes were red-rimmed and swimming. Dried tears lay upon his pallid cheeks. He looked to be in a state of near collapse.

There was one letter, and it was for Natasha. She took it from the post boy and slipped it into the pocket of her blazer, staring wonderingly at the albino.

"Willem! What's the matter?" she demanded.

"Madame, you will come with me, please—yes?" he said in a voice of desperate urgency. The man was so distraught that he was having to lean on the wall for support.

"But what *is* it?" demanded Natasha.

"The *principessa*—she is . . ." the strange Dutchman sketched a vague gesture in the air, and his swollen eyelids overflowed with fresh tears.

"Something the matter with her? Is she ill?" prompted Natasha.

He nodded. "Madame, I am frightened. Please to come. I have the scooter." And he gestured towards an aged Lambretta leaning against the wall by the gate. It had a pillion seat.

Natasha glanced dubiously at the scooter. "But is there anything I can do?" she asked. "Isn't the doctor with her?"

"The doctor?" Willem's eyes widened with something like horror. "I cannot be sending for the doctor, madame. You must be coming, please." He reached out and laid a hand on her forearm, appealingly. "You are an English lady, and you will know what to do. Please."

Something—either the albino's pathetic state, sympathy for the old woman down in the crumbling palazzo, or, perhaps, the naked appeal to her chauvinism—decided Natasha that she must go with him. But—riding pillion?

"Please to mount, madame." Willem was already seated and kick-starting the little machine.

They bowled down the bending hill and into the square, where several of the village men were already playing cards at the café tables. All eyes followed the Lambretta with its ill-assorted riders, till it swept out of sunlight into shade, rounded the basilica, and exuberantly mounted the steep carriage drive before the palazzo. It seemed to Natasha, on dismounting and following Willem to the great front door, that the façade of the building had further crumbled and mouldered since she last saw it.

There was the same smell of decay inside, and a silver tray

of old food—some pasta, plastered to a plate in its own dried tomato sauce, with a piece of broken crust—stood on a side table in the hall. There was a mouse nibbling at the bread; it kept nibbling while they went past it.

"Please to follow me, madame," said the albino, brokenly, leading the way up the wide staircase that led to the old woman's bedroom. He paused for a moment outside the bedroom door, listening with his blond head cocked on one side like a terrier. Then he opened it, and motioned Natasha to follow him into the room.

The window shutters were still closed against the glare of sunlight that, nevertheless, pierced their cracks and crannies, sending thin beams across the room, lighting up the haze of still dust that hung everywhere.

Natasha gagged, and nearly retched, as a sickly smell of stale scent and mildew affronted her nostrils.

"Open the shutters," she said. "And the windows."

"At once, madame." Willem hastened to obey.

The Principessa Adelina Josefa lay, fully clothed in the ankle-length black dress in which Natasha had first seen her, on the ivory-coloured counterpane of her canopied Medici bed, her head propped up against two pillows. The small, plump hands were folded across the slightly protruding stomach. The berry-black eyes were half-closed in the hollows of the old skull. The mouth was open.

She's dead, thought Natasha.

But—not dead. The opening of the shutters sent a blaze of sunlight sweeping across the bed and across the ivory-coloured features of the old aristocrat. Momentarily, and almost imperceptibly, the eyelids fluttered against the glare. Then the movement was gone, and the eyes remained half-opened and unseeing.

Natasha took one of the plump hands. It was cold and moist: ill-feeling.

"I was finding the *principessa* like this when I try to wake her this morning," said the albino, at her elbow. "At first, I think that she is dead." He began to cry again. "She cannot be wakened up. I am trying many times. Please, you try, madame."

"Has this happened to her before?" asked Natasha. "We must ring Dr. Negretti straight away. Where's the phone?"

"Oh, no, madame. Not to get the doctor. All we have to do is to wake the *principessa*. Then she will be all right. You see." He reached forward and began to pat the ivory cheek of the old woman on the bed. "Waken, *principessa!* Wake now! Wake! Oh, madame, you must know so better how to do it— an English lady . . ."

"Leave her alone!" snapped Natasha, snatching his arm away. "Where's the phone. We're getting the doctor here, and no more nonsense."

There was an old-fashioned telephone receiver, of the pedestal type, on a papier-mâché escritoire at one corner of the bedroom. Natasha went over and unhooked the earphone. Remembering having seen such a thing done in period movies, she wound the handle at the base and hoped for the best.

A woman's voice answered hello.

"Please connect me with Dr. Negretti."

Negretti was on the line within a few moments, and he recognised her voice. "Good morning, *signorina*," he said. "No complications with Sr. Yardley, I trust?"

She told him what had happened.

"Not the *principessa*, surely!" cried Negretti, and he sounded amused. "The *principessa* has never been ill in her life. I have never attended her, but it is said she has not even had to have a tooth filled. Can't wake her, you say? I can scarcely believe this, but I will come round right away. Did she complain of feeling ill last night? Ask that Dutch fellow."

Natasha looked round, to obey the doctor's injunction, but the albino had gone. Nor did he answer the front door to Negretti's knock, a few minutes later; Natasha went down to let the doctor in.

And Willem's Lambretta had gone from outside the palazzo where he had parked it.

Dr. Negretti's brief examination resulted in a humming of the telephone wires. The first call was to Naples.

"Barbiturate poisoning, undoubtedly," said Negretti, to some colleague at the hospital. "Secobarbital or pentobarbital overdose. No, it was not prescribed by me. You will be over immediately? Good. Meanwhile, I'll take what supportive measures I consider to be expedient."

"Is she dying?" asked Natasha.

"We are all dying, in a sense," said Negretti, replacing the earphone and giving her his sweet-wry, hunchback's smile. "And now, my dear *signorina*, I think that you should telephone the district *polizia*, while I am doing what I can for my patient."

He met her wide-eyed stare, and nodded.

"If the old lady dies, the police will have to be informed. They might just as well know now, and employ their energies, between now and her possible demise, in discovering the source from which the sleeping capsules came—for they are only to be had on prescription, and the *principessa*, to my knowledge, has not consulted another physician."

Negretti's nurse arrived soon after: an aggressive woman in the habit of some lay sisterhood, who brought an armful of clashing enamel basins and snakish rubber tubing; she bundled Natasha out of the bedroom.

Wandering downstairs, Natasha found herself at the open door of the grey room in which she had first been received by the *principessa*. There was another telephone in this drawing room, and she had the sudden thought to call the *principessa's* friend Ballard, and give him the news. Willy-nilly, she had been gathered into the situation; despite her anger towards the man who had insulted her, it was a small service that she could hardly walk away from.

The woman at the exchange made her connection. It was a long time before Robert Ballard answered. His Midlands accent sounded alien and unattractive; his voice was slurred, and he was either drunk, or very near to it.

"Wassat, eh? What you say?"

"I said this is Natasha Collingwood," she repeated coldly. "The *principessa* is ill and unconscious from an overdose of sleeping pills, and it occurred to me that you should be told."

"Good God! I'll be right over!"

She put down the receiver, as the sound of a police siren's double note died away at the top of the steep street outside.

They came into the Palazzo di Roberti, big-booted and important: two motorcycle policemen outriders, who flanked the inside threshold like praetorian guards, and saluted Pinturicchio as he padded in, soft-footed in rubber-soled corespondent's shoes of black-and-white pointy half-brogue. He looked surprised to see Natasha standing in the hallway —though, surely, the officer who had taken her call at the *polizia* had informed him that she was the informant?

"Miss Collingwood again? Our paths seem to cross with agreeable frequency." His eyes probed at her figure. "What do you know about all this, then?"

She told him of her part in the episode: how the albino had called for her at the Villa Gaspari, and had brought her here.

How it was only on her insistence that the doctor had been called. How he had now disappeared.

"Put out a call for that Dutchman," said Pinturicchio. "The number of his Lambretta's on record. If he tries to get off the peninsula, we'll get him at the road blocks. If he hides out in the hills, it may take days. But he won't get far."

Moments later, there came a crackle of static from a police radio outside. Through the open door, Natasha could see that a fair-sized crowd had already gathered, summoned by all the police activity.

"I should have taken action against that Dutchman months ago, when he first came to work for the old lady," said Pinturicchio. "He doesn't have any real papers. Probably jumped ship in Genoa or Naples, but the *principessa* wouldn't let me touch him. The old aristocracy . . ." he hunched his broad shoulders ". . . they still have plenty of pull in this country, as in yours, I suppose."

"He wouldn't have harmed the *principessa*," said Natasha. "They were devoted to each other." Pinturicchio gave her a sly look, and she felt her cheeks colour up. "I mean, he was the perfect servant, and she appreciated him."

"Time will tell," said Pinturicchio.

The harsh clanging of an electric bell announced the arrival of the ambulance and the medical team from Naples. Young fellows all, they tumbled in through the door with the cheerful enthusiasm of a white-coated football team, loaded down with gas cylinders and medical paraphernalia, and chattering excitedly. Dr. Negretti greeted them from the top of the stairs, and they went on up. The bedroom door closed behind them.

"Let's hope she'll pull through," murmured Natasha.

"I agree there," said Pinturicchio. He paused for a deliberate moment—or so it seemed to Natasha—before he went on: "I have quite enough in the way of unexplained deaths on my hands already."

Natasha felt a sudden trail of icy chillness down the full length of her spine, but when she turned to the inspector, he was pointedly looking down at his fingernails.

Pinturicchio was on the telephone when Robert Ballard arrived in his beat-up VW. The artist was clearly suffering from a king-sized hangover, which he had probably been freshening up when he received Natasha's call. There was a jaundiced tinge to his tanned face, and his eyes were pouched. He appeared to have made a hasty attempt to shave himself, and a small ball of blood-soaked cotton wool was stuck to his chin. Natasha turned her head sideways in distaste as she caught the reek of stale spirits on his breath.

"How is she?"

"I don't know. They're giving her some treatment now."

He glanced swiftly about him: towards the open front door and the two motorcycle praetorians; towards the door of the drawing room, through which was carried the loud, rapid voice of Pinturicchio on the telephone.

"Look—I've got to talk to you!" He took Natasha by the elbow.

She shook him off brusquely. "You've already talked to me, Mr. Ballard! Last night, if you remember!"

Ballard sucked his teeth irascibly. "Don't hand me that stuff," he said. "Don't sound off like some little scrubber of a mill girl who got herself touched up on a coach trip to Blackpool. With your kind of upper-crust county background, you can take a bit of straight talking in your stride. I've heard of the way they carry on in the hunting field. No, honestly, I'm dead serious." And he looked serious.

Natasha eyed him warily. "Go on."

He looked about him again, and then: "I'm not giving this to Pinturicchio. Not yet. It's too hot, and I don't want it to blow up in my face, or anybody's. But the old lady was on to something—about the murders."

"You said murders."

"I meant murders. Susannah and that lad. I think Susannah was murdered and so does the *principessa*. I bet Pinturicchio thinks so, too, if the truth be known. Maybe you do, too."

"I try not to think about it," said Natasha.

"Listen. She told me yesterday, when I came for her sitting, that she thought she had some most remarkable evidence—those were her very words. Now, though we shared confidence in a lot of things—things like the need to warn you that you might be in danger—the old girl was a bit of a tease, who insisted on playing a lot of her cards very close to her vest. I think she did just that with this piece of most remarkable evidence she talked about—and I think that's why she's lying upstairs now, in the condition she's in."

"You mean—someone tried to kill her, with sleeping pills?"

"She sure as hell didn't try to kill herself," said Ballard. "Not the Principessa Adelina Josefa. And there's no question of her accidentally taking an overdose; she wouldn't need to have sleeping pills about the place, not with the kind of good health she enjoyed. She slept like a baby, just as she had digestion like a horse, and caries-free teeth in spite of a lifetime of sucking sugared almonds."

"Willem's run away," said Natasha. "The inspector's alerted all the local police to catch him. Willem certainly acted very strangely. Instead of sending for the doctor, he panicked and came to fetch me on his scooter."

"Willem's scared of the police," said Ballard. "I don't know why. He's possibly got a record somewhere . . ."

". . . and he was terrified that the *principessa* was going to die on his hands and bring the police down about his ears," supplied Natasha.

"Something like that."

"But why come and fetch me, of all people?"

"I can imagine that you inspire confidence among the more gullible type of foreigner," said Ballard, sourly. "The lesser breeds without the law, they always did look up to the memsahib. You would have been a sensation at the siege of Lucknow."

"Why have you told me all this, that you're not telling the inspector?" demanded Natasha.

He stared at her, and she sensed the whole weight of the physical strain behind his drink-inflamed eyes.

"It's the same old story," he said. "I'm trying to impress on you that the best thing you can do is pack your bags and get away from here.

"I think we've got a killer here in our midst. And I don't mean little Giulietta Capucci. He—or she—is laying about him —or her—in what seems an extraordinarily haphazard manner, but there must be some meaningful pattern underlying it all . . ." he gave her a mirthless, lop-sided grin ". . . and the chances are, I'm afraid, that it might encompass you. And that would be a pity, because I've quite grown to like the cut of your aristocratic-looking nose."


"Give me the verdict, doctor." Pinturicchio was quick to buttonhole Negretti at the bottom of the stairs. They were bringing the *principessa* down on a stretcher, and one of the medical team was holding a drip-feed bottle above the still form. The old woman was still unconscious.

"Hello, Aldo," said Dr. Negretti. "You're putting on weight. I shall have to diet you."

Pinturicchio looked long-suffering. "The verdict, doctor, please. Is she going to die?"

"Not of barbiturate poisoning, I think," said Negretti. "But we don't like the condition of the heart. She's an old woman. The overdose imposed a considerable strain, and that could kill her."

"How big an overdose was it, doc? A fatal dose?"

"Degrees of toxicity vary according to the subject and the circumstances, but I should say that the *principessa* ingested at least the equivalent of three or four two-hundred-milligram sleeping capsules."

"When was this, doc?"

"Early last evening, as far as we were able to determine."

"This barbiturate—take it out of the capsule, and what's it like, doc?"

"A white powder. Crystalline, odourless, bitter-tasting. Soluble. And, by the way, she had also taken alcohol last night."

Pinturicchio walked with the hunch-backed doctor behind the men carrying the stretcher out to the waiting ambulance. The steep street down to the basilica was now a sea of watching faces, half in shadow, half in sun.

"Bitter-tasting, eh," mused the paunchy inspector. "What do you think about a couple of these capsules emptied out into a glass of Campari? That's bitter-tasting. Then spike it with gin, maybe."

"Two drinks like that would just about account for it, Aldo," said the doctor, approvingly.

They stood by and contributed a symbolical touch, as the stretcher was lifted into the back door of the vehicle.

"She's always looked so healthy, walking about the village," said Pinturicchio. "Never realised she was so old till I saw her like this. She'll never survive this, surely?"

"One of my first jobs, as a very young and freshly qualified doctor," said Negretti, "was to deliver a baby in this village. The poorest, scrawniest little thing you ever saw—nothing but a pair of noisy lungs and a body like a starved rabbit. I never thought they'd rear the sickly little wretch."

"So?" grunted Pinturicchio.

The hunchback gave one of his quick, illuminating grins and prodded the inspector in the stomach. "So—look at you now, Aldo!" he said.


"My present attitude towards you," said Ballard, "is coloured by my regard for the shape of your nose, and also by the remorse I feel for what I said to you last night. Also by the way you rallied round the *principessa*."

They had seen the ambulance taking the *principessa* down the coast road to Naples. Now Ballard was on the way to drop her off on his way past the Villa Gaspari.

"I didn't even understand what you were driving at," said Natasha. "And I was called a whore again, by someone else, last night."

Their eyes met in the rear-view mirror.

"Were you, now?" said Ballard. "And who else called you that?"

She told him.

"That grubby little cow," said Ballard, without heat. "She's probably even worse than she looks. The mob she hangs around with have been chased out of practically everywhere in the western Mediterranean, from Tangier to San Remo, and it's only a matter of time before they get the heave-ho from here. They're bad. And I don't just mean bad, fun-style, but rotten-bad; the sort of rank outsiders who give permissiveness a bad name."

He slowed the car to a halt at the gates of the villa, and reached to open the door for her. He had a better colour now, though he still smelt of drink. "Do one thing for me," he said.

"What's that?"

"I know we're a long way from being bosom friends, but I'd like you to trust me. Basically, I'm on your side. I think you're in trouble—bad trouble. Promise me, if anything else happens, if you're threatened again in any way, to phone me. All right?"

She nodded. "All right. I'll do that."

"Good for you," he said. And, as Natasha got out of the car and crossed to the gates: "Watch out for that Amanda bird. I could tell you a few things about that one."

And I, thought Natasha, could tell you a few things about her, if I so minded.

But she had already decided to betray the letter—if not the spirit—of the pact that she had made with Ballard; for there was only one person to whom she could rightfully present the awful evidence against Amanda, and that was to her stepfather and guardian.

This she would do right away; she would have done it already, but for having gone to the Palazzo di Roberti.

## 12

Nathan Yardley was sitting up in bed shaving himself with an electric razor when she knocked and went in. There was a transistor on the counterpane beside him; a voice announcing the overseas service of the BBC was cut short as he snapped it off.

"What's happened?" he asked. "Mario was here just now, with the news that the police were at the palazzo, and that you'd been seen going there."

Briefly, she told him.

"Oh, no!" he exclaimed. "Not the *principessa*. She's such an absolute sweetie. Is she dying, then?"

"They're worried about the heart," said Natasha. "She's so old and, I suppose, more feeble than she looks."

"A dreadful business," he said, putting away the razor.

She eyed him speculatively. He looked well-rested, though there were still lines of strain about his eyes. The knee, as well as she could judge under its swathed bandage, seemed to have reduced its swelling.

She took a deep breath, and said: "I found Amanda in my room last night . . ." she deliberately let her eyes slip out of focus, so she should not see the expression on his face, when he turned to stare at her ". . . it seems that she went in to rummage through my drawer, the drawer where I keep my personal bits and pieces."

"She stole from you?" His voice was incredulous.

"She found some snapshots of me—and she burnt out my

eyes with a cigarette end. Like the photo of Susannah that I found up in the graveyard."

"Oh, my God! Isn't there ever going to be an end to it?" He pressed a hand to his brow and closed his eyes. "Are you sure she did it, Natasha?"

"She didn't even bother to deny it," said Natasha. "When I arrived on the scene, she was in the bathroom, having obviously ducked in there with the intention of flushing the snapshots down the loo. She had them already torn up in her hand. When I asked her why she did it, she just . . . abused me."

"I'm sorry, Natasha."

"I felt I had to tell you."

"Of course. Of course." He took his hand away from his brow and leaned back against the cushions, eyes still closed. "Do you have any idea why she did it, Natasha?"

"Yes," she said, in a voice that seemed very small and frightened. "I think she thinks that you and I have started an affair, Nathan, and she hates me for it."

Now she was meeting the level regard of his disconcerting blue eyes. She tried to hold her gaze, but had to look away in confusion. "I can't think of any other explanation, any other reason why she should have said the things to me that she did."

"Sit down, Natasha," said Yardley, gently. "No, sit here, on the edge of the bed, so I can see you. I've got to unburden myself to you quite a lot, and I want to be able to gauge your reactions when my skeletons come tumbling out of their dusty attics.

"In the first place, you're quite right about Amanda. She had the same idea about Susannah and me. Susannah hadn't been here a week before Amanda was abusing her for trying to seduce me, and this was ridiculous, because poor Susannah wasn't attracted to me one bit. Hers was a more earthy taste, for youth and muscle; middle-aged semi-intellectuals didn't come into her scale of sexual attractiveness. But there's more to it than that.

"Amanda's twenty now. In six months' time, she'll come into a small legacy from her mother; then I've no doubt she'll join the eternal peregrinations of that international hippy set she picked up with here this spring. She grew up fast. Too fast. Her mother scarcely noticed what was happening, though, God knows, poor Anna had the burden of her own secret problem that filled almost all of her life.

"The truth about Amanda is this: When she was only sixteen and her mother was still alive, she threw herself at me, her step-father of only a year.

"And one night, here, at the Villa Gaspari, while Anna was sleeping in her own room on the next tier—in the building with the colonnade and the mimosa shrubs—Amanda came to this room, nude under her dressing gown, and cried for me to let her come into my bed."

The skeletons were tumbling out fast. She could see, with compassion, that his unburdening to her was cathartic: For years, he had carried the canker of his secrets inside him. What he told her—calmly, soberly, and without rancour or bitterness—was a shedding of his burden. She felt at once proud and grateful to have his confidences.

The wife—Anna—had been the linchpin in the nightmarish relationship that had grown up between mother, daughter, and step-father. In a quiet voice, Yardley spoke of his early happiness at having taken over a ready-made family—and this at the age of nearly forty, when he had become almost resigned to material failure and the prospect of a lonely old age. Life —suddenly sweet, and further to be enriched by the success of his book—opened out for him and his Anna at the Villa Gaspari. It was an idyll that was swiftly to be blasted apart.

The secret drinking was no secret from him by the end of their honeymoon at the villa. By the time Amanda and Eric joined them in Italy in the school holidays, he had become well-practised in the art of covering up for Anna. The children, who had been at boarding schools since the breakdown of their parents' marriage—when Anna had turned to drink—never knew what was going on, nor were ever to know.

For him, he said, there came a revulsion. At one stage—while he was in a depressed state, after hearing that "Tell Me Another" was going to be shut down—he seriously considered walking out on Anna. She—who may or may not have still loved him, but who needed him more and more, as her sickness took an increasingly stronger hold on her—pleaded with him to stay on any terms he liked. He stayed—and moved into a separate bedroom, the one he was in now, leaving her the suite of rooms on the tier above, with the colonnade and the mimosa shrubs.

With the worsening of her condition came a deeper rift between them, and a greater revulsion on his part. Natasha listened with horror to the end of it: how the desperate, dying woman had played her last card to hold the only man in the world upon whom she could lean.

It was with her mother's connivance, possibly, and certainly with her knowledge and complaisance, that the young Amanda had offered herself, repeatedly, to her step-father—and had been gently but firmly rejected.

Sometime during the unfolding of the story, he had taken Natasha's hand in a firm grip. The story done, he relaxed his hold so that she could quite easily have slipped her hand away. She did no such thing. And it seemed just right.

"I'm so sorry," she said, "that you had to tell all that to me. If I'd known, I would have kept the business about Amanda and the photographs to myself. I—I suppose she must still be terribly jealous and possessive of you."

He nodded. "Yes, but don't run away with the idea that she's in love with me, or even infatuated, any longer. All that very quickly turned to loathing, when she felt that I'd spurned her. After her mother died, she twice ran away. I had to get her back, of course. It would have been much better if her own father could have been persuaded to take her, but he's too busily engaged in chasing showgirls. She stays. Her hate festers. You took some of the brunt of it, because—as you rightly assumed—she thinks there's something between you and me. I don't know how it's all going to end."

Natasha leaned forward and kissed him on the brow. It was a companion gesture to that which he had made to her the previous night: chaste, affectionate, honest.

"You look worn out," she said. "The talking must have tired you. Is the knee paining you very badly?"

He nodded. "Natasha . . ."

"Close your eyes and get some rest, and I'll go and organise something to tempt your appetite for lunch." She looked at her watch. "It's eleven o'clock. I'll waken you at twelve-thirty with a pre-lunch martini. How will that be?"

He tightened his grip on her hand, so that she had to pull gently to free herself.

"You're too good to me."

"Rubbish."

"Natasha . . ."

She paused at the door and looked back. "Yes."

"Are your two sisters as beautiful as you are?"

"Go to sleep, Mr. Yardley," she said, fondly.

The view from the terrace included the colonnaded building with its urns of mimosa, and it was to this that her eyes were compulsively drawn. It was there that Anna Yardley had spent her last days on earth; there, with her mind and morals shredded and flattened by the drink that was killing her, she had schemed to entrap and hold onto her husband by using the nubile body of her own child. Natasha shuddered, though the sun was hot upon her arms and shoulders.

There was no one about: The Capuccis were all preparing lunch in the kitchen; neither Eric nor Amanda had appeared all morning. A small motorboat was shaping a course towards a headland dominated by a ruined fort that lay beyond the bay in which the village stood. She followed its mackerel-patterned wake, till the craft disappeared from her sight beyond the headland. She even counted up to a hundred beyond that, before she moved.

She bowed to the impulse—the sudden obsession—to see into Anna Yardley's quarters, to trespass in the place where the other woman had once lived, dreamed, despaired, and died. No one would see her; no one would ever know.

The colonnaded building stood apart on its own, and was reached by its own flight of steps, that branched off from the main steps a short distance from the door to Nathan Yardley's room. Shedding her sandals, she went up them, barefoot and silent.

Beyond the colonnade, there was a green-painted double door set in an oval archway. She gently depressed the latch. The door was locked.

There were two oval-topped windows each side of the doorway, complementing its shape, and they were closed and shuttered. Peering through the slats of the nearest window, Natasha could just make out the interior of what appeared to be a dressing room. There were dust sheets over some of the furniture, but she could see a dressing table and mirror, a chaise longue draped with a leopard skin, and several chairs.

There was an armchair directly in front of her vision, its seat facing in the opposite direction, the high back of the chair turned towards her.

She addressed herself to the problem of getting into the colonnaded building by other means than the locked front door. It did not take her long to discover a possible way.

One end of the building, which presumably contained the bedroom, faced the sea. Simply by going back half-way down the approach steps, she could look up and see that there was a wrought-iron balcony overhanging a steep drop to the rocks above the beach, and there were french windows out onto the balcony. One of the glass doors was partly open, and a long net curtain stirred in the slight breeze. A wide stone moulding ran out over the edge of the drop, to form the base of the balcony. At the cost of two or three hair-raising steps, she could win her way to the balcony and that open french window.

The short distance along the moulding was worse than she had anticipated: It took an age of shuffling steps, eyes fixed firmly on the warm stonework three inches from her face, and no hand-holds. It was a blessed relief to feel the edge of the balcony under her fingers, and the work of a few instants to climb over the wrought-iron balustrade and tip-toe to the open window.

Anna Yardley's bedroom was in pink shadow. Dusky pink carpet, pink-flowered wallpaper, gossamer pinkness of chiffon swags descending from the bed canopy. There was a painting on the wall beside the bed, and she crossed over to examine it: Her bare feet made no sound on the thick-piled carpet.

It was a half-length portrait of a woman in a lilac negligée, seated at a dressing table. A beautiful woman, with the same blue eyes as Eric and Amanda; they were turned towards the viewer with an amused and slightly mocking expression that echoed the tip-tilted edges of the lips.

"Anna—Anna Yardley." Natasha whispered the name aloud.

The mother's resemblance to her two children was very marked—except for one particular: Instead of the butter-yellow hair, hers was a head of auburn curls, dressed with a studied negligence.

*At that moment, Natasha heard a sound coming from the next room.*

Even as her eye measured the distance to the french window, and her mind came to grips with the problem of winning her way out to the balcony and beyond it; even while her bloodstream was taking its new infusion of adrenalin for swift movement, she saw, from the corner of her eye, that the handle of the door leading into the dressing room was beginning, slowly, to turn.

Fear of being caught in the embarrassing position of an intruder was instantly ousted from her mind—and replaced by an instinctive awareness of peril.

Flight would not come. As in a nightmare, she stood rooted to the spot, desperately willing her limbs to obey her screaming nerve-ends. She looked around for something to use as a weapon—but there was nothing.

The latch of the door snicked open, and a slender hand came into view. Then the sleeve of a lilac negligée.

It was shadowy in Anna Yardley's pink bedroom, and the more so over by the door, which lay beyond the limit of the thin sunlight that was admitted by the curtained windows; so that, when the door was fully opened, and the figure came into view, the face was still insubstantial. An insubstantial face—under auburn curls of studied negligence.

"Who—who are you?" Natasha recognised, with some difficulty, that the voice was her own.

No answer. The apparition came across the room and into the line where the sunlight began: first the slender feet in feathered mules, then the skirt of the flimsy garment, the deep vee at the neckline, and the hint of bosom. The face. The face—white and staring-eyed with fury, reddened mouth gaping—was the face of young Eric Yardley.

"What are you doing amongst my mother's lovely things?" The boy's opening words, and the vehemence with which they were spat out, shocked her so that she could only stare. He looked taller, more powerful, than she had noticed before.

"No one comes in here but me!" he mouthed the words with such violence that spittle ran down his chin. "No one—not even Nathan—is allowed in here except me." The neckline of the negligée had fallen farther apart, and she could see a lacy brassière, obscenely padded, spanning his lean chest.

"I'm sorry," she managed to falter.

"Nothing in here's been moved since the day she died," said Eric, gesturing round the room, "and I come here every day, when I'm at home." He looked sly. "I tell them that I'm working in my room, but I really come here."

"It's all . . . very lovely," murmured Natasha.

"My mother was a very lovely lady," he said. "She was perfect, like a saint. No one could ever come near to taking her place. And no one's going to." He came closer to Natasha, and she saw a rivulet of sweat trickle out from under the auburn wig and course down his neck. "Have you been copulating with Nathan again this morning? I saw you go in there. I know you do copulating with him. You did it yesterday afternoon. That's what made me so mad with you."

She shook her head, helplessly, fighting to find the words to get through to him. "Eric, you're so wrong. You don't understand . . ."

"I know what you're trying to do," he said. "Susannah was just the same, but I jolly soon stopped her. I scared the pants off old Susannah, I did. Ha!"

They were both about the same distance from the door into the dressing room. Was the outer double door bolted, or locked with the key in place? Natasha began to edge sideways, away from him.

"Tell me more about what you do in here, Eric," she said, placatingly.

"Mostly I just sit and think about her," he said. "Sometimes, I take some of her lovely things out and look at them. There's plenty to do in here. And nothing's been touched, only by me, since the day she died."

Three steps to the door of the dressing room. She could see the dust-sheeted furniture, the dressing table and the chaise longue, all striped in sunshine and shadow from the shutterings. In the centre of the line of oval-topped windows was the double door leading to the outside. There was a large key in the lock. It might work, she thought, simply to cross into the other room, unlock the door, and walk out. She glanced again at the boy—and thought better of the idea.

"Show me more of your mother's things, Eric," she said. "Show me the other room. It looks so elegant. She must have been a person of great artistic taste."

"Her clothes are all in there," he said. "All in racks. There are furs and silks and things. All very soft. They smell of her scent. I remember her scent for as long as I can remember being alive; the earliest thing I can remember of her is the way she smelt when she bent over to kiss me good night."

He walked into the dressing room, teetering awkwardly on the high-heeled mules, and Natasha followed him, determined to position herself, as soon as possible, between him and the outer door.

He slid back the door of a built-in wardrobe, and she saw a line of hanging clothes, polythene-shrouded all, all in muted tones of lilacs, greys, and fawns.

"Fifty pairs of shoes," said Eric proudly. "She had fifty pairs of shoes. Some of them hardly worn, and not two pairs alike."

He seemed calmer, more self-absorbed: His attitude was that of the curator of some obscure museum, where people seldom came, and where the treasures within are only lovely and meaningful to the one whose task it is to show around the apathetic visitors. Natasha edged two steps backwards towards the door, her hands behind her.

"No one else will ever wear these lovely things but her," said Eric, ruffling along the row of whispering chiffons, silks, and velvets. His eyes panned to meet hers. "No one, do you hear? Neither you, not that Susannah, nor anyone else!"

Natasha looked about her, desperately. "This is pretty," she said, pointing to a china figure that stood on a low papier-mâché table. A moment's serious inspection revealed it to be nothing more than a cheap piece of fairground junk: a crinolined lady embellished with stuck-on glitter, made in some sweatshop in Hong Kong. But she could scarcely have made a better choice as far as Eric was concerned. He beamed happily.

"That was my very first present to her," he said. "When I was only a kid. It didn't cost very much. I bought it from a sort of antique bazaar, with my own pocket money. But she treasured it, and never went away without packing it in her bag."

"Oh, Eric," said Natasha, suddenly disarmed. "What a lovely thought."

"Don't you touch it!"

She had already picked up the figure when he cried out; she was still only holding it between forefinger and thumb, by the smooth shoulders, when he made a grab at the thing.

The crinolined lady slid out of her grasp, fell past the edge of the papier-mâché table to the floor—and was decapitated on the table edge, in passing.

"You meant to do that! You did that purposely!"

He was at her then, hands at her throat. And his hands were big and hard. The rouged and kohl-smeared face was close to hers, and he was crying tears.

"You broke my mummy's lady, you horrid old cow!" he screamed at her.

Eric's strength—to her unspeakable relief—was not the strength of madness; only the muscled power of a well-nourished fifteen-year-old. She shook him off—with some difficulty. He collapsed on his knees beside the table, clutching at the broken china figure.

There was a hammering at the door.

"Eric! Eric, I can hear you in there. Open up!" Amanda's voice.

Natasha unlocked the door, and came face-to-face with Amanda, who was wearing a beach dress, and dark glasses that did not conceal the fact that she must have had a sleepless night. Her shrouded gaze slid past Natasha to the grotesquely garbed figure inside the room.

"Good God! You've been getting yourself up again," she said. "Oh, Eric, how many times have you promised me you wouldn't?"

The boy rose to his feet, his face suddenly washed of expression; childlike, vulnerable. He looked down at himself. As if for the first time, he seemed to notice the state of attire he was in. With a cry of alarm, he covered his thin chest with both hands and rushed into the bedroom. The door slammed behind him.

"Well, you've seen what he is," said Amanda, dully. "And I suppose you'll find it good for a laugh with your sedate friends, when you get back to London. I take it you *are* leaving. Despite what Eric says, there really can't be anything of a permanent nature going on between you and Nathan, can there?"

Natasha shook her head, bemused.

Amanda took a crumpled packet of cigarettes from her pocket, put one to her lips, and swore when her first match failed. "I'm sorry about last night," she said. "I found that little sod Eric in your room, doing those creepy things with your photos. When I asked him why, he came up with this big lie that you'd tried to seduce him."

"Me? Seduce Eric?" said Natasha.

"On the hill, on the way up to the procession, he said. He's such a chronic liar, I never would have believed him for one moment, but I was having a bad scene. I'd been popping pills that Bimbo gave me, and my skull was turned inside-out. There was just enough left of my brain to make me kick him out, and to start flushing the evidence down the loo when I heard you coming up the steps."

They could hear Eric moving about in his mother's bedroom.

"Did he do those things to Susannah's grave?" asked Natasha.

The girl nodded. "I can hardly believe he tried to dig her up, but he must have done. He had this thing about Susannah: that she was going to marry Nathan and roll around all day in mother's underwear. It drove him to killing her dog. Oh, yes, he did that—I forced him to admit it. Did he kill your kitten? I don't know. He probably did."

"He's very sick," said Natasha.

"Mother's death left him high and dry," said Amanda. "He was at school in England when she died, and after she was buried in Naples, we got the news that he'd run away. That was the first time he bolted. He did it three times after that, and was expelled for that and other reasons—the headmaster who did the last sacking was too much of an old maid to reveal Eric's particular crime on that occasion. In the end, no decent public school would have him. Now he goes to a special establishment that charges the earth, provides the outer trappings of an upper-class education, and keeps poor little sods like Eric under some kind of physical restraint that the parents don't probe into too deeply . . ." Amanda stubbed out her unfinished cigarette, nervously, with the toe of her sandal, on the doorstep. "There's one thing you should get clear, though: His cruelty to animals doesn't extend to murder. I mean people-murder."

"Last evening, someone in the religious procession made a clumsy attempt to push me to my death," said Natasha, evenly.

"I knew he'd got a hate on for you," said Amanda. "That's why I tried to get him home when I saw you both together. But was it a real, honest-to-God attempt to kill you, or only to put a scare into you? And are you sure it was him who did the pushing?"

Natasha repeated the admission she had made to Nathan Yardley, about her heightened nervous state at the time. "And I hadn't seen Eric for quite a time, though I was calling out his name," she added.

"I'll get the truth out of him," said Amanda. "I can handle him, and so can Nathan. You'll have gathered that Nathan and I don't get on; but I have to admit that he's good to Eric."

There were, obviously, unsuspected facets to the character of Amanda Neville-Yardley.

"What will happen to Eric when he grows older?" asked Natasha. "When he doesn't have you or Nathan to watch over him, to anticipate what he's going to do; when he no longer goes to this—what did you call it?—special establishment?"

Amanda fumbled for another cigarette. "I dunno," she said. "I try not to think about it too much. God, I wish Mummy were alive. It's no wonder her going broke Eric apart so completely. She really was a wonderful, complete person. We're diminished without her—both of us."

On an impulsive prompting, Natasha asked: "Amanda, what did your mother die of?"

Amanda looked at her in mild surprise. Her blue eyes were brimming with tears; Natasha had never seen her look so much like her brother.

"Why, of cancer," she said. "She'd suffered from it from just after the time when she remarried."

She left them, the brother and the sister, in their dead mother's shuttered apartments—and went down to the dining room. It was approaching twelve-thirty, and time to wake Nathan with the pre-lunch cocktail that she had promised him. Bottles and glasses were laid on a side-table, and there was fresh ice provided in a covered container.

To go—or to stay?

She poured a measure of spirit into the mixing bowl, and considered the question. Nathan Yardley had used his need for her in his work, to urge her to stay—and that consideration was still valid. Aside from that—though he had not invoked it, and she had enough basic integrity not to make it her prime cause for staying—there was the debt of gratitude she owed him for furthering her career. No, she could never forget that.

Then what else? What about the attraction she felt towards him? Or was it simply the mawkish heart-flutterings that even the most sensible and level-headed women feel about men who are famous, distinguished, and—presumably, in Nathan's case—rich? What about the feelings, if any, that he might have for her? Here she was on less safe ground, having no point of reference. Or do over-forty best-selling authors have a tendency to fall for their secretaries? Certainly, in Nathan's case, the proposition seemed to be contra-indicated: His regard for Susannah had seemed to add up to a rather weary acceptance of her secretarial usefulness balanced against her sexual carryings-on with all and sundry (Had she ever had an affair with Robert Ballard?); and his manner with herself, Natasha, had been—despite the lurid imaginings of poor Eric—impeccably correct, though undoubtedly friendly. He admired her —yes, there was no doubt about that.

The problem of Eric—and the things that she had just learned about that unhappy boy—had also to be taken into account, in the decision as to whether to go or stay. . . .

Absent-minded in her task, she slopped a little of the mixture onto the top of the rather nice marquetry table. Prompted with wayward thought that it might stain, she put her hand into her blazer pocket for her handkerchief—and came upon the letter that she had received that morning: the letter that a succession of events had driven from her mind. It was from her friend and flatmate, Veronica.

With the intention, merely, of skimming over the salient points of her friend's communication (for Veronica was sometimes trivial as to content, and always long-winded), she ripped open the envelope and quickly read the familiar, neat typescript.

It was the last page of Veronica's letter that carried the shock that blasted her out of the orbit of destruction to which she had become bound—albeit loosely bound—in the Villa Gaspari.

## 13

The first six pages were composed of a protracted account of Veronica's scanty social life since their parting after breakfast on the previous Wednesday morning: Veronica—asthmatic, timid, and painfully aware that men didn't find her attractive —made what shift she could of the outer fringes of parties, and other people's conversations and flirtations.

The seventh and last page dropped straight into her first reference to Natasha. Veronica had been to a party given by one of the directors of the high-toned, graduates-only secretarial agency with which they were both enrolled, and she had picked up an intriguing titbit of gossip:

. . . Miss Fildes, who had been at the sherry, asked if I had heard how you were getting on. When I said no, she treated me to a certain amount of nudging and winking, and when I looked rather blank, the old dear told me what you probably know already.

Despite the last-minute panic, it seems, your Mr. Yardley actually started looking for you about two months ago. Had the agency scour their books for the right candidate; not interested in anyone over twenty-five, and he wanted to see photographs. Miss F. was drooling into her sherry glass like some old, old procuress when she said: "I knew dear Natasha would get the appointment if beauty was the criterion —and I was right."

So, dear. Tell auntie. What are his intentions? I do hope

they're not entirely dishonourable—though I envy you in any event, with that dishy man. . . .

Natasha read it through to the end. Veronica's slightly malicious teasing was hardly important, nor was the fact that Nathan Yardley had chosen his new secretary with an eye to her appearance—any man would do that, given half a chance.

What was important was that Nathan Yardley had lied by omission. Susannah Hislop had suddenly given a month's notice only a few days before her tragic death. Yardley—who freely admitted that he owed so much to Susannah—had never given the slightest intimation that he had already selected her successor, Natasha, a whole month before that.

It was a circumstance, she told herself, that probably had an absurdly simple explanation. But, on the way to see Nathan Yardley and tackle him about it, she grew less convinced.

The newly made dry martini she left on the table in the dining room—where the midday sun through the window quickly turned the frosting on the outside of the glass to a little puddle of water at its base.

The smell met her nostrils as soon as she walked into his bedroom: an indefinable smell that she had come across somewhere before; the memory of it lurked somewhere on the outer limits of her consciousness, but she could not find the association to recall it.

Yardley had not acknowledged her tap. Assuming that he had limped into the bathroom, she had gone straight in.

On the tousled bed lay his transistor and the green leather-bound notebook. Nothing else in the room but the faint tang of his cologne—mingled with the strange smell to which she was unable to put a name. From behind the closed door that led to Yardley's bathroom and dressing room, she heard the sound of running water.

Absently, she began to straighten the bed: plumped up the cushions and picked up the transistor and notebook, placing them on the side table. The thick notebook fell open in her hand at the centre pages. It was of fine bond paper, faintly ruled, and the pages were numbered consecutively in type; exquisitely bound, it was the sort of luxury item that one would expect to find among the intimate possessions of a famous author, along with a monogrammed propelling pencil in gold, perhaps, and an inkstand of carved jade; a tool, for all its beauty, with which an artist could perform his sober, dedicated task of creating form.

Natasha flipped to the first page of the notebook and turned several more pages. She was staring down at them—and trying, unsuccessfully, to assimilate what she found there—when Nathan Yardley came back from the bathroom. He wore a short towelling robe, and the bandages were sliding below his injured knee. His eyes flared with something like alarm when he saw her there.

"What is it?" he said. "What's the matter, Natasha?"

She turned and tossed the notebook back on the bed. The whole thing was going to be more difficult than she had thought.

He limped across the room and took hold of her arm. The smell of his cologne was very strong: He must have just put some on.

"What's the matter? Have you heard something?"

Again his acute sensitivity to atmosphere: There was no concealment from the perception of an artist. Dully, she took Veronica's letter from her pocket. Avoiding his eyes, she detached the last page and gave it to him: It seemed the best way.

"I had this from a friend," she said.

She turned away while he read it through: crossed over

to the window and looked out over the gulf. The white upper-works of a big ship were riding, like a mirage, above the far line of the horizon, and she was absently trying to determine which way the vessel was moving when she heard his laugh. It was a sudden explosion of a laugh that was like a sudden release of tension, and there was something else expressed in it: relief.

"Good God, Natasha," he cried, "is *that* all?"

She looked at him: All at once there didn't really seem very much for her to say.

"All right, all right," said Yardley. "I lied to you, when I told you that Susannah gave her notice to quit. I fired her. I had to. She . . ." With one hand on the footboard of the bed, to support himself, he sketched a gesture with the other. "I had to get rid of her, Natasha. She was making life impossible. I can't begin to explain to you the situation she put me in."

"You were her lover?"

"Along with all the others. Intermittently. Yes," he said. "I'm sorry I lied to you about that, too."

"You didn't lie about it," she said quietly. "Not in so many words. You said that she wasn't attracted to men like you—middle-aged and a semi-intellectual, you said."

He groaned and smote his hand on the footboard. "God, Natasha, I can't remember what I said. Does it matter now? Listen . . . I've got something to tell you . . ."

"No—please—listen to me. It's rather important." She took a deep breath, to control her voice, which was beginning to waver with nervous emotion. "Aside from Amanda, at least two people in this village believe that I came here to be as much your concubine as your secretary. I didn't understand at the time, and it didn't really matter . . ."

(Did it not really matter? . . . that Pinturicchio and Ballard had thought her—probably still thought her—to be a whore?)

". . . it didn't matter, because it wasn't true. It still isn't true. And your relationship with Susannah concerns no one but you and her—and certainly not me—so that makes no difference to the way I feel; except that, taken in conjunction with all the dreadful things that have happened here at the Villa Gaspari, it makes me want to get out of here."

"You're leaving because you've found out that I was having an affair with Susannah."

"That's not true," she said. "Not true at all, and it's unworthy of you to make such a crude and simplistic reading of my motives. I'm leaving because I find myself in a false situation that's got progressively worse since I've been here. Now I want out."

"You're angry because I lied to you—because you've learned that I'd already searched for a new secretary and made arrangements for you to come here, before I told Susannah she'd have to go."

"No. It's not like that."

He lurched towards her, and nearly stumbled, so that she had to reach out her hands to steady him. Then he was holding her by the shoulders. Again it came to her: the strange smell that she had met on first entering the room. It came from him, and it lay behind the tangy scent of his cologne.

"Don't leave me, Natasha. Don't ever leave me. Let's go away together. Now. Today. Away from here, and away from the whole rotten business . . ."

"You're hurting me." She struggled to get out of his grip, but his hands were too insistent, too powerful.

"South America, darling. We could live there, really live. We could fly out today. There's nothing to keep us. Natasha . . ."

"Let me go!"

His moist mouth was at her neck, and his hands swarming

down her back, to imprison her waist. She drew away from him till there was no farther to go, and she was against the wall, imprisoned in his grasp.

"She never meant anything to me, Natasha. I swear it. She was detestable. Detestable! When she found out about you —that you were coming—she screeched like a bloody fishwife . . ."

It was important, now, not to resist. His mouth was doing things to her throat, to her cheeks, and to her lips that had to be endured; like his questing fingers that were kneading the small of her back.

"Why did you tell her about me?" she whispered, falsely. "That was an awfully silly thing to do."

"I didn't tell her. The bitch found the correspondence with the agency. She'd had herself a key cut for my private drawer."

He was still nuzzling at her throat; she forced herself to relax and go with it.

"So that's why Susannah committed suicide," she said. "Because of me."

The moist mouth paused, and she felt herself to be poised on the edge of eternity.

"I couldn't stop her," he said. "She threatened it, but I never really believed her. As I told you, I thought she wasn't the type. Oh, my dear, let's not talk about it, not now. There'll be so much time for explanations—but not now."

He released her, and held her at arms' length; and she deliberately unfocussed her eyes so that she should not see the expression in his, so that his face was only an oval blur.

"You will come with me, won't you, darling little Natasha?" he said, softly. "You'll make everything worthwhile, and I can make you so happy. There's a great, wide world of freedom waiting for us, with everything we need for the rest of our lives. I've got a fortune put away in a South American bank.

No one will be able to touch us—the gossipers, the muck-rakers, the scandal-mongers. You *will* come?"

She made herself smile. "Can I pack a few things?"

He hugged her. "Hurry. Hurry. Then come back and help me."

Natasha slid past him to the door. Something made her turn and glance back at him, from the threshold. He looked very old.

She ran up the steps and out of the gates of the Villa Gaspari. There was a ramshackle country bus that had stopped fifty yards farther up the road in the direction of Amalfi, to pick up an old man and woman in black. She raced to it before it moved off again.

It was on the way to Amalfi—while staring out of the bus window at the illimitable blue of the sea beneath her—that fickle memory provided, unbidden, the key of association relating to the smell in Nathan Yardley's room.

Some years before, in her early teens, while on Christmas holiday from school, she and her brother Joe had gone on a shopping expedition in Cambridge; and there, in one of the big stores, they had got stuck in a lift between floors. No one in the crowded compartment thought anything of it—till there was a jolt, and the lift fell a few, terrifying feet down its shaft; then hung for nearly an hour, until rescuers forced a way in and brought everyone up. In that crawling hour —while Natasha silently made sundry specific promises to God regarding the future conduct of her life (contingent upon that life being spared), some of which she kept, and while women and children screamed—one person alone, in the lift, remained outwardly calm.

He was a little man in a shabby overcoat who stood with his back to Natasha, face turned to the wall. She was pressed quite closely to him, so closely that her cheek lay against his shoulder-blade. And during the course of that interminable hour, she became aware of a strange smell issuing, so it seemed, from the coarse fabric of his overcoat: a smell that grew stronger as the time went by; sweet-sour and pervasive, and quite unlike any body odour she had ever encountered before.

The thump of the rescuers' rope ladder on the roof of the lift, which brought a fresh chorus of screams from the trapped people, also caused the little man to look round sharply, and Natasha saw his face for the first time. She saw the face of a man in such mortal terror as to be beyond screaming, beyond thought, almost beyond living. And she knew that the smell that came from him was the smell of naked fear.

It was this smell that had met her when she had first come into Nathan Yardley's room—before she ever showed him the letter.

And—now that she thought of it—the expression on his face when he had seen her standing in the room was not unlike what she had seen in the face of the little man in the lift all those years before.

She was sitting at an outside table of a smart café in Amalfi: blue-and-white tiled floor, gay umbrellas, and a view over the sea wall to the shallows, where *la jeunesse dorée* were at play with their speedboats and their water-skis. Youth—and simple innocence—suddenly seemed a long way away.

There was a man opposite her, also at a table on his own: a middle-aged Latin with gold-rimmed spectacles and an imperial beard and moustache. He inclined his glass towards her, and his fleshy lips made a false smile of gallantry; but his resolve broke against her impassiveness, and he found it important to blow his nose. She, on the other hand, was relieved when a newsboy came by. Did he have an English paper?

"*Si, signorina. Grazie, signorina.*" The lad left with a good tip.

Natasha opened up the copy of the *Courier* and hid herself behind it. How many days had gone by since she last looked at a newspaper?—yet nothing seemed to have changed: The middle spread was given over to a picture feature on the Frenchwoman who had had stillborn sextuplets; the President of the republic had ordained that she should be decorated, and she and her husband looked very happy with the surrogate offspring of their union.

Shut out the sight and the touch . . .

The sight of Nathan Yardley and his naked fear, as he stood framed in the bathroom door, with the bandages beginning to slide below his injured knee; the lurching, awkward way he came towards her, so that there was so question of stepping aside; the feel of his hands, his lips.

Shut out the sounds. Oh, yes! . . .

Thank heaven she was not flying today (but tomorrow?), because there had been, overnight, one of the classic air disaster horrors, and this took up almost the entire front page: a low-level, aerial view of an airliner strewn over a palpably English landscape, with its liveried tailplane impaled upon a palpably English oak—and, for good measure, a close-up of a helmeted English bobby pointing up at the thing in the tree.

*NINETY NUNS PERISH IN RELIGIOUS CHARTER FLIGHT*

The sounds were not to be shut out. . . .

Nathan Yardley's hastily assembled explanations—or lies— after she showed him the letter. Thinking on his feet—surely he should have been better at it than that, the star of "Tell Me Another"; he had lied to her with more glibness on other occasions. What had happened to throw him off balance?

The bearded Latin was getting to his feet and dropping a

pile of coins by the side of his empty glass. Natasha raised the
edge of her paper higher, as protection against a possible in-
trusive farewell.

Nothing else on the front page save a small item about Red
China: that there was some easing of the tension between her
and the Western powers, it said, was evidenced by this morning's news of . . .

A shadow fell across her, and a hand fell on the back-rest of
her seat. She looked up with a start. Because his head was
silhouetted against the sun, she did not at first recognise Robert Ballard.

"I came right away," he said. "But why in God's name didn't
you ring before? What have you been doing since you left the
villa?"

"Walking about, mostly," she said. "Trying to sort it all out."

"What have you had to drink?"

Puzzled, she motioned towards her half-empty glass of
aperitif. Ballard clapped his hands and snarled to a waiter,
who came running.

Not till she had downed the brandy that he ordered for her
did he break the news:

"Yardley's dead! The Capuccis must have found him after
you left. The police are looking everywhere for you."

The late afternoon brought clouds and a ruffling of the surface of the sea. The beautiful young people abandoned their
water skiing, put on exotic finery over their swimsuits, and
trailed up the stone steps to where their cars were waiting.
None of Amanda's crowd seemed to be among them.

"Was it suicide?" Natasha asked.

"He was found under your window," said Ballard. "Under
Susannah's window, on the spot where she died. No one's told
me how he got there. Another drink?"

"He killed her," said Natasha, dully.

"Susannah? You must be joking. What would a fellow like Yardley kill a bird like her for?"

"He killed her," she said. "I know he killed her. Out of all the rigmarole of lies he gave me, he also said that she committed suicide because he was planning to get rid of her and bring me here. But that was simply a lie that I offered to him. And he took it."

"Listen," said Ballard. "You're out of your mind to believe such a thing. I knew Susannah pretty well: I did some drawings of her, and had the almost unique distinction of being one of the very few adult males in the district who didn't lay her. There wasn't anything about Susannah that could possibly have motivated him to kill her. She was an easy-going, not-very-bright, idle trollop."

"Idle?" asked Natasha, puzzled. "But he told me—and I remember it quite well—that she was a tremendous worker. That was her great virtue. She drove him on to finish the book."

"She was bone-idle, and didn't care who knew it," said Ballard. "She used to laugh about it when she came to model for me (in the nude, of course; I couldn't keep the clothes on her): how she'd been slung out of, I think, fifteen jobs in four years before she came to work for Yardley."

"But—why should he have lied to me about that?"

"To justify his keeping her, I expect. But I promise you that, as far as work was concerned, he'd not have got more than a bit of simple copy-typing out of Susannah—and unwillingly, at that. And she was so ignorant that it hurt. Yardley could only have put up with her because she was a convenient lay—a fact that he'd hardly have been in a hurry to acquaint you with."

"Yet you think—thought—that I was her replacement, in every sense," said Natasha.

"Briefly, I did," he admitted. "But I changed my mind."

"Why?"

"You know why. Forget it. I'm sorry. As to Yardley killing Susannah, I repeat that he had no possible reason for doing so. If he tired of her, all he had to do was to fire her—and a nice fat cheque would have sent her on her way rejoicing. Little Susie's horizons were strictly bounded by bedsheets, and she worked from one man's mattress to the next, with no regrets."

A police car rolled to a halt at the kerb nearby, and two officers looked out at her. She recognized one of them as the young constable from the village *polizia*.

"They've come to take you in for questioning," said Robert Ballard. "But don't worry. I'm coming with you. As I told you this morning, we've had a murderer in our midst, and I think you were threatened. Let's hope the whole thing will be wrapped up. People just can't go on dying like this."

The murderer's dead, thought Natasha. He died of a mortal fear that came to him some time between eleven o'clock, when I left him, and twelve-thirty, when I came back.

There were four of them waiting in the cemetery. The two workmen had rigged up a screen round Susannah Hislop's grave, and were now leaning on their shovels, sucking at home-rolled cigarettes. Pinturicchio and Dr. Negretti paced up and down the path leading to the gates. Rizzio was waiting outside the gates; every time his superior came into view, he shook his head and spread his hands in a gesture of helplessness.

"Aldo, you worry too much," said the hunch-backed doctor. "You live on your nerves. Coupled with your excess weight, this is a pattern for disaster. Unless you change your way of life, you'll have heart trouble before you're forty."

The late-afternoon overcast had spread across the peninsula.

The two walkers cast no shadows, but Pinturicchio was sweating badly.

"Have you had any leave this year?" demanded Negretti.

"I was due to go last week," replied the other, sullenly, "before this business came up. I had to stay and see it through. There was no one I could turn it over to. There was so little to go on, you see? Not much more than an instinct."

"You knew this girl? This Susannah Hislop?"

"By reputation. I fancied her, all right, but I wasn't one of those who went with her, if that's what you mean. It's not easy for a policeman."

"And you decided she didn't die accidentally."

"It couldn't have been an accident! Listen, doc, I had one of the typists from headquarters at Amalfi try it time and time again: walking past that window—only we had the shutters closed for safety, of course—with bare, wet feet. She was the same size as the Hislop girl—not too tall—and the window sill came well above her knees. Even when she simulated a slip of the foot, she had no difficulty in grabbing the window frame. Add to that, the tiles are practically non-slip: Rizzio, the typist and I must have padded around for half an hour in our bare feet, trying to fall over."

"Suicide, then?" asked the doctor.

"I never believed it," said Pinturicchio. "Not having seen that girl around, and the way she carried herself. She loved that body of hers too much to destroy it. No—it had to be murder, for me."

"And now, you're in trouble, Aldo."

"The Ministry wants to know why I've kept the case to myself for a week. There's talk of a disciplinary enquiry. If this latest thing falls flat, I shall solve my weight problem, never fear. They'll have me back in uniform, on foot patrol."

"But why did you keep it to yourself?" probed Negretti.

"You even kept it away from the press, and you might have known that would mean trouble for you when the reporter fellows from Naples found out."

"It's all very well for you," said Pinturicchio. "Even as a country doctor you meet up with the whole range of things that lie within the compass of your profession: childbirth, disease, death."

"I think I know what you're going to say, Aldo," smiled Negretti.

"Ten years," said Pinturicchio. "Ten years I've been a policeman, and I've never dealt with anything more out of the ordinary than knife fights between drunken fishermen. And now—this. Murder, with foreigners involved and a famous name . . ."

He was interrupted by a whistle from the gates. Turning, they saw Sergeant Rizzio gesturing excitedly towards the steps behind him.

"At last," said Pinturicchio. "The fellow from the Ministry. Now we shall soon know if there's anything in it."

The newcomer was tall, well-barbered, and wore a dark-coloured lightweight suit that gleamed in silken folds. He was fortyish, possessed a good figure, and had a manner that was coldly alien. Pinturicchio docketed him—sourly—as Milanese.

"This caused a great deal of trouble to obtain at such short notice," said the newcomer. "And it is to be hoped that you will be able to justify your demand for an exhumation, Inspector." He took from a crocodile-skin briefcase a printed document. "We were not entirely clear as to the reason for your request. There was some evidence given to you—was this sworn evidence?"

"Evidence from a prisoner in custody," said Pinturicchio. "Given voluntarily, this afternoon."

"Name of the prisoner?"

"Giulietta Capucci."

The man from the Ministry made a pencil notation on the corner of the document. "You can now give orders for the exhumation to proceed, Inspector," he said. "There is a doctor present?"

"I am a doctor," supplied Negretti.

"Indeed?" The man stared pointedly at Negretti's hump.

Negretti winked at Pinturicchio, and they walked off together towards the screened grave.

"What a bastard," growled Pinturicchio. "You see what I'm up against, doc. Do you need me around when you open up the coffin?"

"It will be unpleasant," said the other, "and there's no point in upsetting yourself if you're not used to this kind of thing. Better if you stay and ingratiate yourself with our friend."

Pinturicchio pulled a wry face, but was glad to turn back when the doctor went behind the canvas screen, where the grave-diggers were already at work with their picks and shovels.

The man from the Ministry was stalking slowly round the outer path of the cemetery and gazing at the larger of the mausoleums with a studied detachment. Pinturicchio joined him and offered him a cigarette, which was brusquely refused. They walked together, under the sentinel cypresses; the detective felt compelled to alter his step to conform with that of his companion—and cursed himself for what seemed like an admission of inferiority.

Time passed . . .

"They don't seem to be hurrying themselves!"

"There are some concrete blocks to be lifted out," explained Pinturicchio. "That will slow them down."

For the umpteenth time, they turned together at the far end of the cemetery, and the other consulted his gold wristwatch.

"I have to catch a flight for Rome this evening."

"I'm sorry," said Pinturicchio. And he really felt sorry.

Presently, the sound of the picks and the shovels ceased. As one, the two men paused in their perambulation and looked towards the concealing screen.

"I should think they'll be opening it up now," said Pinturicchio.

The other made a brusque gesture with his well-manicured fingers, motioning him to silence; then groped for the silk handkerchief in his breast pocket and brought it, tentatively, towards his nostrils.

Dr. Negretti came round the canvas screen a few moments later. He waved to Pinturicchio.

"Did you find anything?"

Negretti was carrying something. It turned out to be a discoloured envelope. The detective moved swiftly forward and snatched it from him, slit the flap with his thumb, and took out the contents: two sheets of smooth-coated paper that felt oily to the touch. Photostats.

He opened up the sheets and found himself looking down at a copy of a piece of typescript:

### Chapter One

I've lain under the Southern Cross with a nut-brown maid, seen the Sugar Loaf towering out of the sea of mist of Rio Bay, blown three months' salary in one night of Monte Carlo, been broke in Cochin, pissed up against the Golden Gates of Samarkand. . . .

"It's a photostat of what looks like the original typescript of Yardley's famous book," said Pinturicchio, with a dull feeling that something had gone badly amiss. "Corrections and all. But why . . . ?"

He turned it over. The second sheet was a title page, again in typescript:

### THE FALL OF THE PROUD
*a novel by*
*Wallace Oswald Spurgeon*

The rest of the page was covered with scrawled pencil notes in a backward-sloping, female hand.

"Who is Wallace Oswald Spurgeon?" snapped the man from the Ministry, who was reading over Pinturicchio's shoulder.

But a great light was falling into the life of Aldo Pinturicchio, and he had no reck, any longer, for the might and panoply of his faceless masters. He had the answer ready, and this was his triumph.

"W. O. Spurgeon," said Pinturicchio, slowly, so as to savour the effect on his listeners, "is a British businessman who has been held, without trial, by the Red Chinese, since 1970. This morning, it was given out that Peking had announced that they were considering the release of two out of three Britishers whom they are holding. At midday, it was announced on a radio newsflash that all three men had, in fact, been passed over the border into Hong Kong . . ." he looked about him, scanning their faces for signs of comprehension ". . . and I don't doubt that Nathan Yardley, who had possibly heard the earlier announcement, certainly heard the second and—what was to him—fatal piece of news!"

The face of the man from the Ministry which, at close quarters, was narrow-browed and weak about the mouth, remained obstinately uncomprehending; but Dr. Negretti's lively countenance was creased in a smile of pure delight and admiration. And he was clapping—as for a good tenor solo at La Scala.

"Splendid, my dear Aldo," purred the hunchback. "Truly splendid. I am so proud to have delivered you into the world!"

## 14

A pretty nursing nun brought them to the *principessa's* private room, along a glass-walled corridor that self-consciously looked out onto a picture postcard panorama of the Bay of Naples, from the black pyramid of Vesuvius to the Isles of Ischia. She tapped on the door, opened it, and stood meekly aside for Natasha and Ballard to go in.

"You will please stay only thirty minutes," she murmured with a firmness that belied her sweet face.

The *principessa* was propped up against the pillows with her white hair drawn up under a lace cap, and a brocade bed jacket draped round her petite, plump shoulders. She looked like a tiny, bright-eyed Victorian doll in a glass case in some museum. Willem was sitting with her, dressed in a white linen suit, and smiling to show his gold inlays. He bobbed to his feet and bowed to Natasha.

"Such a naughty boy," said the *principessa,* and she took the albino's hand. "He hid up in the mountains, and the inspector had such a task to find him. However, it has been a blessing in disguise. We . . ." she gestured to them both ". . . had always thought that poor Willem had accidentally killed one of the rough sailors, which was why he ran away from his ship and came to serve me at the Palazzo di Roberti. Happily, we now know that the man recovered. Place a seat for Miss Collingwood, Willem. How are you, my dear? And how is my friend Mr. Ballard?"

"How are you, more like?" asked Ballard gruffly.

The old woman smiled. "In the future, I shall choose my company more carefully before I accept cocktails."

"We found sugared almonds in Naples," said Natasha. "Violet-coloured, the sort you prefer."

"So kind, so kind," said the *principessa*. "Perhaps Mr. Ballard will stop glowering at me and pass them round."

"You've been holding out on me," said the artist. "I thought we were accomplices—but you told me hardly anything of what's been going on at the Villa Gaspari all these years."

The old woman slipped a sugared almond between her fine teeth and smirked.

"You knew more about Yardley than you ever let on to me," persisted Ballard.

"His late wife I knew well," said the *principessa*. "I came to know her after she bought the Villa Gaspari with the ample alimony from her first marriage. I was her confidante when she fell in love and married for the second time. Later, I was her confidante in sadder matters."

"What was she like—Anna?" asked Natasha.

"She was the wittiest and wisest of women," replied the *principessa*. "She bore with fortitude a second bad marriage— and a sentence of death."

"He said—Nathan Yardley said—that she killed herself with drink," murmured Natasha.

"To have said such a thing to you was one of the wickedest things he ever did in a wicked life. Sometimes, when she came to see me, we would have a little aperitif, no more. I never saw her drink heavily. Cancer killed her. Negretti will tell you."

"Why did she marry that rat?" demanded Ballard.

The *principessa* spread her tiny hands. "I am in no doubt

that he thought she was rich, but her family made no provision for her, and her alimony ceased with her remarriage. Still, there was the Villa Gaspari."

"He told me that he married to get roots," said Natasha. It seemed to her that there was no end to the deviousness and perversity of the man who had been Nathan Yardley.

There was more, much more . . .

It was not hard to imagine the two women—the dying Anna and the aged aristocrat—sitting together in the dusty grey drawing room at the Palazzo di Roberti, while the younger poured out her agonised confidences; confidences that, let it be said, the *principessa* had kept till both of the parties concerned were dead.

Yardley, the compulsive liar, was also a compulsive seducer. Even in his seductions, he was devious and perverse—and his wife had been witness to most of them. He who, after his fame as a TV personality of the highest orbit, could have had any woman for the asking, first required that his women should be in love with him. To this end, it was his technique to lead them through a maze of lies and counterfeit emotions, teasing them—and himself—in a protracted mental orgasm.

It was then that Natasha saw the subtlety of his campaign with her (for, in the light of the *principessa's* account, there was now no doubt in her mind that Yardley's careful selection of her from the agency candidates had been a preliminary to seduction): how the kindling of her sympathy by the story of his own near-failure had led gently and naturally to his offer of help in her career. We artists have got to stick together! She felt suddenly cheapened—and her poor, honest, and long-dead ambitions filthied—by the recollection of it. Then there was his accident. What a godsend that had been to him, that air of suffering and the Byronic limp. How much more quickly had he been able to insinuate an air of easy intimacy between them: the little candle-lit suppers *à deux* in his bedroom. What a fool she had been.

"He deceived me completely," she said aloud. "I began to fall for him, like some silly, impressionable schoolgirl."

"Do not chide yourself, my dear," said the *principessa*. "He was a man of great skill in persuasion. I recall my friend saying that she scarcely believed the evidence of her own eyes when she saw him manipulating other women. And remember that she—who was also a person of clear-eyed intelligence, like yourself—was so taken in as to marry him. That poor creature, what she suffered before her end. While on her deathbed, she had to watch him turn his attentions to her own young daughter. Is it to be wondered at that the child has turned out so badly?"

"He told me," said Natasha, slowly, "that his wife gave Amanda to him, to keep him with her."

The *principessa* spread her hands. "Do we need further proof that the man of whom we speak is far better off dead? May the good Lord forgive me for asserting so."

The arrival of the pretty nun, with a draught of medicine for the patient, provided an interruption. As she walked out, she looked pointedly at her watch, and then at Natasha.

"Tell us what happened on Saturday evening," said Ballard. "You went to see him, didn't you? Without telling me, Willem, or anyone. And nearly got yourself killed in the bargain."

"You are a terrible tyrant," giggled the *principessa*. She sought confirmation from Natasha: "Is he not a terrible tyrant and bully?"

"Why did you go? Why?" demanded Ballard.

"Miss Collingwood could answer that," said the old woman, "but I think she was not paying complete attention when she came to see me at the palazzo. We talked of the book—the famous book—and I put a question to her."

"I vaguely remember," said Natasha. "You told me that you had begun to read it in the Italian translation."

"I asked you, did you not think that the tone and style of the book was quite unlike anything you would expect from a man of his character and temperament," said the *principessa*. "In this I was, as you say, drawing a bow at a venture, since I could hardly have expected you to know him so well, and, indeed, I did not know him sufficiently well to form such a judgement; I was only acting on the judgement of his late wife. Imagine my surprise when you agreed with me."

"I—I'm afraid I misheard the question," said Natasha, embarrassed—remembering that she had been speculating on the *principessa's* possible relationship with her young albino man-servant at the time.

"Damned if I can remember it either," said Ballard. "Was that before I arrived? Yes, I suppose it was—more of your keeping things from me."

"My apologies, fellow-gossip," purred the *principessa*. "I admit it—I asked Miss Collingwood to come early, so that I could sound her views about the book."

"You guessed that he hadn't written it?" asked Ballard. "You really had hard cause for suspicion. Why?"

"On two counts," said the *principessa*, ticking off on her plump little fingers. "First, the character of the book vis-à-vis the character of the supposed writer. Setting aside the literary value of this book, upon which I am not competent to pass judgement, I would say that it is—if it is nothing else—a very straightforward and honest book. I would say that its author is a very straightforward and honest man, and his character shows through the very first pages, like a light through a lantern-glass. This was the face that that evil man turned to the world; indeed, in the few little chin-wags I had with him, this was the impression I had of him: straight-forwardness and honesty. But my dear friend, his late wife—with the directness of people of her nation—once told me that he was a two-faced, cut-glass phoney!"

"He was the complete deceiver," said Natasha. "There was a beautiful green leather-bound notebook, in which he told me he'd written thousands of words towards his new book. When I opened it, the day he killed himself, it had nothing but a few pages of doodles."

"I take your point," said Ballard. "But I can understand why the *principessa* kept it to herself. It wasn't hard evidence. A man can be a supreme creative artist and still a phoney. Richard Wagner was a phoney. Anything else? You mentioned two points."

"Second," said the *principessa,* touching her second finger, "there is the evidence of the House of the Pristine Moon." She looked, with a smile, from one to the other of their puzzled faces.

"Explain yourself," said Ballard.

"The House of the Pristine Moon is—or was—an eating house in Nanking. It is not the sort of establishment that would be known to tourists, being discreetly situated in a quiet part of the city, and catering exclusively for local palates of discrimination. My father and I, when we travelled to China and visited Nanking, were taken there by a mandarin gentleman. In all probability it no longer exists in its original form."

"So?"

"The House of the Pristine Moon—lightly disguised by the name of the House of the New Moon—appears in the book, when, you will remember, the hero is in Nanking. Now, I knew that the man who claimed to have written that book had never been to China, because I once asked him. How, then, was he able to describe—in particular detail, so that I, who went there sixty years ago, recognised it immediately—an obscure but beautiful establishment in the capital city of Kiangsu province?"

"He could have lifted it out of a book of reference," said Ballard. "What am I saying? Hell, he lifted the whole damn book!"

"That is what I set out to prove—or disprove—when I called to see him," said the *principessa*. "I walked to the villa by way of the beach, to save myself the fatigue of the hilly road. There was no one about. I heard the sound of television coming from the kitchen quarters. There was a light in his apartments. I knocked . . ."

Natasha shuddered.

"And . . . ?" prompted Ballard.

"He received me very agreeably," said the old woman. "We talked for a while of matters literary. I was very careful, very discreet."

"So damned careful and discreet that he decided you were too dangerous to live!" exclaimed Ballard.

"I think I pressed the point about the House of the Pristine Moon too persistently," said the *principessa*. "He had never heard of the real name; told me that he had drawn the place entirely from his imagination. This, of course, I knew to be impossible. Later, when I returned to the subject, he must have realised his blunder. He offered me a drink. He mixed a very good gin and Campari—so I accepted a second. He had to go out of the room to mix the drinks. I was very foolish."

The young nun swept in.

"You will all go now, please. The *principessa* will sleep."

They made their good-byes, and the *principessa* took Natasha's hand and whispered close to her ear, nodding towards the albino, who was backing towards the door, bobbing his head and smiling back at them.

"He is such a good boy. There are many who would misunderstand. We are very devoted. The inspector says he can remain in Italy. It is a great relief to me—for comfort's sake."

"I'm so glad," said Natasha. "Really glad."

Pinturicchio was down in the great plate-glass-and-tiled entrance hall of the hospital. With him was Sergeant Rizzio. They both got to their feet, and the uniformed officer saluted Natasha.

"Waiting to see the *principessa*," explained Pinturicchio, probing her figure with his eyes.

Thinking of the young nun, Natasha privately speculated that he would be in for a long wait.

"Any news of that chap who really wrote the book?" asked Ballard. "Spurgeon, or whatever his name is."

Pinturicchio seemed keen to communicate. He waved them both to easy chairs set round a low, glass-topped table, and offered cigarettes.

"Spurgeon is being flown back to London," said the inspector. "It is the biggest news-story of the year, and the news media are going wild about it. [Pinturicchio himself appeared on the front pages of all the Naples newspapers that day—as the local whizz-kid who had cracked the case.] He made a short statement to the Hong Kong police, and I was sent a copy."

There was no doubt about it—the big man was positively preening himself, and Natasha speculated—and not for the first time—on the popular fallacy about people being mellowed by success.

"I can't understand how Yardley worked the fraud," said Ballard, "or how he hoped to get away with it."

"Simpler than you might think," said Pinturicchio. "According to Spurgeon's story, he met Yardley at a party in London, while he was home from China on sick leave—he suffers from a weak heart, which hasn't been improved by the rigours of his imprisonment. Yardley had been championing the cause of unknown artists and writers on the television, and Spurgeon told him about this book—he called it *The Fall of the Proud*—that he'd written. Yardley took the typescript and promised to read it. Two weeks later, Spurgeon went back to China without having had any reaction from Yardley. Almost immediately upon his arrival there, he was arrested. So much for how. Now we come to why . . ."

"That would be just before his TV show folded," said Natasha. "He knew what was coming, and the idea of returning to obscurity must have been a nightmare to him."

"It's a pleasure to work with you, Miss Collingwood," smiled Pinturicchio, regarding her with the air of a man who has unexpectedly become the owner of a talking horse. "You are so perceptive."

"Thank you," she murmured.

"So we have Yardley facing unemployment and obscurity," went on the inspector. "In his possession is a book that was written by a man—a very sick man—who has been imprisoned in a far-off and hostile land, possibly for life, which, in his case, promises to be short. I think we may assume that Yardley changed the title, and submitted the book to a publisher without committing himself as to its authorship, just to get a reaction. We know the reaction he received."

"It was still a hell of a risk he took," said Ballard.

"I think he found it easy to take the risk," said Natasha. "I'll tell you something, Robert: He had the capacity for complete self-deception that all real deceivers possess. Do you know,

when I first met him, he cried real tears of pure pleasure because I sincerely praised the book."

"The book became his," said Pinturicchio. "Miss Collingwood's right—he took complete possession of it, and he killed
to keep it."

Sergeant Rizzio's boots squeaked as he stirred at his superior's elbow, where he was standing. "First: Signorina Hislop,"
he prompted.

"Hislop left a complete account of her part in the business,
on the photostat of the title page that we found in her grave,"
said Pinturicchio. "She found the two pages of Spurgeon's
original typescript quite by accident, at the time when Yardley was copying a few pages in manuscript from it, every day,
and passing it to her to type out."

"So she blackmailed him with it," said Ballard. "Of course!
She always had too much money, and too many model dresses,
for any secretary."

"In the end, Yardley proposed a cash settlement in return for
the two pages she had purloined, and her resignation,"
continued Pinturicchio. "The money was agreed, and the exchange made. Yardley had already arranged for Miss Collingwood to succeed Hislop—and then Hislop blithely told him
that she still possessed a photostat copy, and that she'd no
intention of ending her comfortable position of mistress-*cum*-
blackmailer."

"And that's when he killed her," said Ballard. "He must have
been mad with fury. What a bitch! She had the stubborn, low
cunning of the truly stupid."

"What did she do with the photostats?" asked Natasha.

"For safety's sake, she gave them in an envelope to Giulietta
Capucci," said Pinturicchio, "simply because the girl cannot
read English. She told Giulietta it contained something of vital
importance. That much—and no more—we know from what

Hislop wrote on the photostat. I wonder why she wrote it? Perhaps she realised, despite her stupidity, what a dangerous game she was playing."

Rizzio's boots squeaked again. "Next came Guido," he said.

"Guido was Giulietta's lover," said Pinturicchio. "This morning, she was sufficiently recovered from the shock of his death to give us a statement. She carried out her obligation to Susannah Hislop by placing her vitally important envelope in the dead woman's coffin, before it was screwed down. It was the typical action of the superstitious peasant. Afterwards she told Guido what she had done. She says that he knocked her down and called her a fool. Next thing we know, Guido has tried unsuccessfully to dig up the coffin during the night."

"Then he went to Yardley," said Ballard.

"He didn't know what was in that envelope," said Pinturicchio, "but he had been numbered among Hislop's lovers, and she must have boasted to him that she had some hold over her employer. That night when Giulietta went down to the beach for her assignation with Guido, he had already met Yardley—and Yardley had silenced him with a kitchen knife. The girl didn't know what had happened; she never connected the envelope with Yardley, and Guido never discussed it with her—if there was to be any profit in it, he didn't intend to share it with the mother of his unborn child."

"But—she knew about the envelope in the coffin," said Ballard. "Why didn't Yardley silence her, too?"

"Because he didn't know she was involved," supplied Natasha. "Guido would simply have said that Susannah had given him certain documents, and how much were they worth?"

Pinturicchio's glance was now frankly admiring.

"Miss Collingwood, it really is a privilege to enjoy the clarity of your intellect," he said.

## 15

The Villa Gaspari was a house under siege. They had come from Naples and from London and New York. The big agencies were there, the great dailies, and all Europe's TV. Even the people of the village, released from their canon of arcane behaviour by the sheer size and ebullience of the alien invasion (so different, they were, from the annual influx of tourists: it was reliably rumoured that a woman who had worked at the villa before the Capuccis, in Sra. Yardley's time, had been given a refrigerator for her story, and her daughter a part in a film)—even they were packed, in solid, black-garbed phalanxes, behind the reporters and the photographers, the cameramen, the sound technicians, the boom men, and the clapper boys. Watching. Waiting.

Pinturicchio had provided Ballard's beat-up VW with a motor-cycle escort back to the village. This officer took them straight through the crowd, forcing a pathway through to the other uniformed men who stood guard on the gate, past the importuning media-creatures.

"Miss Collingwood, isn't it? Would you like to say a few words to our viewers?"

"Exactly what was your relationship with the murderer, Miss Collingwood?"

"Hold it, beautiful!"

"Just one more, Natasha!"

"Would you give a thought to endorsing our deodorant, Miss Collingwood?"

"Don't you push me around, ya wop bum!"

The gates closed behind them, and the voices outside sounded like the boom of angry bees. The Capuccis were lined up on the terrace: mother, daughters, and grandfather, all smiling; and the girl Giulietta held her budding stomach proudly. Natasha's suitcases were packed and standing ready, just as she had asked.

"I must go and say good-bye to Amanda," she said to Ballard.

"I'm sorry about Amanda," he said. "I had her written in as the killer—though I have to admit it was largely because of the company she keeps. Don't be long, Sasha. Your plane leaves in an hour and a half."

She was half-way to the steps down when she realised. She turned.

"I haven't been called that since I was a little girl," she said. "No one's called me Sasha since then."

He grinned. "We'll work on it," he said. "It could catch on."

The wind from the sea was bending the tips of the cypresses—the same wind that brought the waves riding right up beyond the shingle. The sky was heavy with overcast, promising a storm.

She paused by the oleander shrub: Looking down, she saw Amanda stalking slowly along the shoreline; she was wearing a long skirt, and her blond hair was covered by a shawl. Natasha called her by name, and the girl turned and waved when she saw her.

They came together by the rough stone wall at the top of the beach.

"I packed your things myself," said the girl.

"Thank you."

"How's the *principessa?*"

"She's going to be all right."

"Good. And now—you're going?"

"Aren't you, Amanda?"

"The inspector took Eric to the airport," said Amanda. "And that was rather nice of him. He'll be all right there. We're going back to Heathrow together on an evening flight."

"Pinturicchio doesn't know about Eric," said Natasha. "About what he did. As far as the police are concerned, all the things that happened to the grave were done by Guido."

"Thank God for that. That's one less problem. And I have to tell you that it was he who tried to push you over that wall. I got it out of him. I was wrong, I'm sorry—he is dangerous to people."

"What are you going to do, Amanda?"

"Get a job. Nursing, I expect. That will come in useful. Sooner or later—unless they take him away and lock him up—looking after Eric is going to be a full-time chore, and I might as well pick up all the expertise that's going."

A sudden gust sent the spindrift against their faces, and the cypresses swayed wildly.

Natasha said, "You can't throw your life away. It isn't fair."

But Amanda was not listening. "I love this place," she said. "Nathan loved it too, do you know that? I think he married mother because she owned the Villa Gaspari. Eric loves it too, and that was a bond between them. For all that he did, Nathan was always very kind and understanding towards Eric; made excuses for him, pretended he was normal. Me—he treated like all the rest."

"Amanda . . ."

The girl's sea-blue gaze turned to her.

"Don't you see that my life's already over?" said Amanda, with the patient gentleness of someone explaining a difficult proposition to a child. "It began with Nathan. He made me alive—turned me into a woman. And now he's gone, and I'm already dead with him.

"Perhaps, in the years to come, when I'm very old, I shall still be able to come back here and be in love again—just as I am now. Good-bye, Natasha."

"Good-bye, Amanda."

They kissed each other's cheeks. Then Natasha left her staring out to the grey sea, and went up to where Robert Ballard was waiting for her.